Until Today

Until Today

Pam Fluttert

Second Story Press

Library and Archives Canada Cataloguing in Publication

Fluttert, Pam, 1971-, author
Until today / Pam Fluttert.

Issued in print and electronic formats.
ISBN 978-1-927583-16-6 (pbk.).—ISBN 978-1-927583-17-3 (epub)

I. Title.

PS8611.L883U58 2013   jC813'.6   C2013-903869-8
C2013-903870-1

Edited by Kathryn Cole
Copyedited by Uzma Shakir
Cover by Jenny Watson
Designed by Melissa Kaita

Printed and bound in Canada

Second Story Press gratefully acknowledges the support of the Ontario Arts Council and the Canada Council for the Arts for our publishing program. We acknowledge the financial support of the Government of Canada through the Canada Book Fund.

ONTARIO ARTS COUNCIL
CONSEIL DES ARTS DE L'ONTARIO
50 YEARS OF ONTARIO GOVERNMENT SUPPORT OF THE ARTS
50 ANS DE SOUTIEN DU GOUVERNEMENT DE L'ONTARIO AUX ARTS

Canada Council   Conseil des Arts
for the Arts   du Canada

MIX
Paper from
responsible sources
FSC
www.fsc.org   FSC® C004071

Published by
SECOND STORY PRESS
20 Maud Street, Suite 401
Toronto, ON M5V 2M5
www.secondstorypress.ca

To all of my fellow survivors,
who I know have the courage and strength to find their day.
Also, to my wonderful daughters, Karlyssa and Shalyn,
who I hope will always make the most of every day.

Chapter One

"Some things just never change around here," my mom says from behind me. I wonder how many times I've heard her say that.

"What'd I do now?" I turn around, holding the musty box I was trying to fit into the back of our SUV. "Give me a break – at least I'm out here helping."

Does she think I'm having fun helping her pack and repack all my brother's stuff? I could think of lots of things I'd rather be doing.

"Katrine, it can't be that difficult to get everything in properly the first time." Glaring at the pile of boxes, Mom swipes a wisp of hair out of her eyes.

I hate it when Mom uses my real name; it always means

she's ticked off. She grabs the box out of my hands and frowns at the mess inside the SUV. Her blonde hair is pulled back from her flushed face, except for those few wisps that have escaped her ponytail. Even with a frown and a red face, she still manages to look pretty. I feel like the ugly duckling standing beside her, with strands of hair plastered to my face and neck.

It's unusually hot for the beginning of September and we're both sweating from packing Jared's stuff. I'm tired, hot, and sick of hearing about his upcoming university adventure. Lucky me – I'm stuck here for a few more years.

"I really want to get this done before your father gets out of the shower," Mom says.

Of course, get it done before Dad has a fit because we messed up his neat piles. "It's not my fault that Jared's so disorganized. He keeps bringing out more stuff."

Mom sighs. "I know, Kat." She puts an arm around my shoulder, making me even warmer. "I just can't believe that he's leaving for university already. You guys are growing up so fast."

A pool of sweat builds on my shoulder where her arm is resting. My throat burns from fighting back tears. She can't make me feel any worse about Jared's leaving. My control is melting as fast as ice on hot asphalt. Squirming out from under her arm, I run toward the house, swiping at the tear that manages to escape.

The house is so quiet, and he hasn't even left yet. Jared adds the excitement and commotion to our home. He does three or four different things at once and always has friends over. Mom is wrong…some things *are* changing, just not the things that should.

My little sister, Sarah, is watching another Disney movie in the family room. It must be nice to just sit there and ignore all the craziness around here. I finally find Jared in the kitchen where he's busy eating, as usual.

"You know, maybe Mom's right when she says some things never change." I punch Jared in the shoulder. "We're slaving out there in the heat for you, and you're sitting in the air-conditioned kitchen stuffing your face."

Jared flashes one of his irresistible grins. Well, that's what some of the girls at school say about his smile. It must be true, since my annoyance begins to fade. "Ah, but things *are* going to change. Mom is wrong this time. I'm going to have the time of my life at university."

Yeah, things may change for you, but definitely not for me. A chill creeps up my back, giving me shivers.

"What's up, Kat? You can't be cold in this heat."

I force a weak smile. "It must be the air-conditioning because I'm so sweaty."

"Hey, Champ! You ready? We really should hit the road soon." Dad swaggers into the kitchen, his hair wet from the shower. I can think of no better way to describe the confident stride of my broad-shouldered father. Jared inherited Dad's build and dark, good looks. Sarah and I are pale and fair, like Mom.

"Yeah, in a minute. Let me just finish my sandwich." Jared stuffs another bite into his mouth. I can't believe he can fit so much food in there at once. It's a wonder he doesn't have a trophy in his room for eating. He seems to have one for everything else.

"Mom's still trying to find room for everything. Jared brought out some last-minute stuff *again*." I look pointedly at my brother, whose only response is a shrug and a sandwich-stuffed smile.

"What? I'd better get out there. She'll never get everything to fit properly."

Dad's attitude is so annoying that I fail to bite my tongue in time. "She's handling it just fine. She doesn't need your help."

Dad glances at me and heads toward the door of the kitchen, mumbling about the attitude of the Thompson females.

I'm about to tell him exactly how controlling he can be, when Jared – forever the peacemaker – jumps in. "Dad, relax. Mom has it under control, or Kat and I never would've come in. Grab some food. It's a long drive."

Dad pauses and grins at Jared. When hasn't he listened to Jared? "You're right there, Champ. I might as well make myself a sandwich. We have to wait for Greg and Amy, anyway. They're on their way over to say good-bye." He turns toward the family room to yell at Sarah. "Hey, Princess, come and have something to eat before we go."

Greg. Just the mention of his name flips my stomach. I run past Sarah to escape outside.

Struggling to keep my lunch down, I gulp fresh air,

managing a few deep breaths before sprinting to our clubhouse down by the river. The sound of my feet hammering against the ground matches the rhythm of my pounding heart.

The familiar smell of damp earth, old wood, and musty curtains in the old clubhouse takes the edge off my panic.

The little hideaway is hot and muggy. I open the small window, and push the curtains aside. I remember how proud I was when Mom hung those frilly yellow drapes. I was only five or six. Jared was so upset that they had frills. I could count on one hand how often I got my way over my brother's.

A small breeze wafts through the window, but it's not enough to fight the muggy air. I grab one of Jared's old baseball bats and jam the door open with it. A peek outside tells me nobody is coming, so I move the stack of milk crates away from the wall and grab my little black book from its hiding place.

The familiar feel of the journal in my hands calms me, and I sit down at the old, wooden table that my dad made for us. The table and chairs seemed so big when we were younger, but now my knees almost touch my chin when I sit. Dad insists on leaving it here for Sarah, but she's not interested in playing in the clubhouse like Jared and I were.

Sarah is different and likes to do her own thing or hang out with Dad when he's around. The clubhouse basically belonged to my brother and me while we were growing up. Jared's baseball bats, soccer balls, footballs, baseball mitts, and other sports equipment litter the floor and shelves, even though Jared hardly sets foot inside anymore. My skipping ropes, tea sets, dishes, and Barbie stuff are still in the plastic milk crates that I just moved away from the wall. Dad used to duck in through the door, sit on the floor and play with me when I was younger. That hasn't happened for a long time, not since Sarah came along and replaced me as Daddy's little girl.

My fingers trace over my name. When I was eight, Jared thought it would be fun to carve our names in the table. He said that it would be something people would be able to read in the future to know we existed…like a caveman's drawing on the wall of his cave. Who was I to argue with my big brother? Jared's name is scrawled across one whole side of the table – as large as possible so everybody will remember him. My name is scribbled into one little corner. Scott and Steph, my best friends since we were kids, have their names on the table, as well as a few of Jared's buddies.

Our father threatened to add our names to a tombstone after he saw what we had done. He told us we had to look after things and respect our belongings, especially after the hard work he put into building that table for "a bunch of ungrateful kids." We can laugh about the whole scene now, but at the time, I was afraid he would never talk to me again.

The memories fade when I glance at my journal. It contains so many other memories…some that I wish would go away forever. I open the book and stare at a blank page for a moment before picking up my pen.

Sunday, September 3.

Jared is leaving today. What am I going to do without him here? I feel so lost and alone. He's always been able to make me laugh when I've needed it. He's kept me sane and protected.

He'll be leaving soon. We're just waiting for Greg and Amy to get here so they can say good-bye.

Why do we have to wait for YOU to come? Why do YOU have to come? Why can't YOU just stay away?

I HATE YOU! I WISH YOU WERE DEAD!

The last word on the page smears as a single tear falls.

Chapter Two

I stare at the ugly words on the page. *Is it true? Could I hate you that much?*

I swipe at my tears and continue writing.

I feel like a bad person for hating you so much, which doesn't seem fair. You make me do things I don't want to do. Was it my fault you did those things to me? Is there something wrong with me that I don't like your touch? I don't think so, but I'm just not sure of anything anymore.

Do I really wish you dead? Sometimes I wish you weren't part of my life and would stay away from my family. You're Dad's best friend and supposed to be like a trusted uncle to me.

Trusted uncles don't do the things you do. Trusted uncles keep their hands to themselves.

You confuse me. Some days I want you to be that uncle, like when you and Amy took us to Disney World. Those times were great and I felt closer to you than to my own dad. I managed to forget about the other person you are. But now it's getting harder for me to forget.

More and more lately, you're the bad Greg, the one who hurts little girls. You've been hurting me and touching me since I was small, using force and threats when I cry and say no. I'm losing the Uncle Greg I used to love to the Greg I hate. I don't even know if I should be fighting this battle inside me anymore.

I don't know who I am. Am I the scared wimp who is afraid to stand up to you, or am I the girl who wants to fight what you're doing to me?

"Kat, are you down there?"

I jump up, knocking over the chair in my haste to get to the window. Scott and Steph are walking across the lawn, toward the clubhouse. Stashing the book behind the milk crates, I can feel my heart beating furiously at almost being caught writing about Greg in my journal.

Scott ducks his head under the doorway and peeks inside. "You're right, Steph. She's in here." Scott grins. "You have to stop hanging out in here. I won't fit much longer."

He has shot up over the last year and is already taller than his dad. Sometimes it doesn't seem right having this big Scott in the clubhouse. All my memories are of a much smaller boy who would always tease and torment us. Scott was a lot like Jared when we were younger. But now that he wants to be a veterinarian, he has a more serious side.

Steph, the complete opposite of her twin, is carefree and takes things as they come. She's the most disorganized person I've ever met and has no idea what she wants to do with the rest of her life. Scott and Steph look alike with their wavy brown hair, brown eyes, and dark complexions, but that is as far as any similarity between the two goes.

Steph peeks around Scott. "What's up? You should be spending time with Jared."

I shrug. "I just needed a break."

"You okay?" asks Scott.

"Yeah. Why?"

Scott looks pointedly at my hands. I try to stop fidgeting and smile, but it feels more like a grimace. I put my hands behind my back, where they can't be seen.

"Yeah, I'm okay." My thoughts whirl furiously as I try to forget about Greg and carry on a normal conversation. "It's just kind of nuts around here. My control-freak dad is driving everybody crazy. Mom finally told him to get lost and have a shower. She's annoyed because I'm not perfect like her. Sarah's just sitting in front of the TV in her own little world. As for Jared…he's too busy stuffing his face to help with anything."

I catch my breath. *Stop rambling, or they'll read you like a book.*

Steph laughs. "Sounds like a typical day in the Thompson household to me."

"Kat, we're leaving!" Mom's shout rattles me. I dread having to say good-bye to my brother with Greg watching every move I make.

Tears pool in my eyes. "I guess this is it."

We walk across the backyard, Scott's arm draped over my shoulder. "It'll be fine. You can call him, and he'll be home to visit."

"I know, but it's not the same. I don't think it'll ever be the same again." I look over my shoulder for one more glimpse of the clubhouse. The Private – Adults Keep Out sign that Jared and I painted in red and black letters still hangs crookedly above the door. *The next time Jared steps in there, he won't be one of us. He'll be one of those adults the sign tries to keep out. Some things do change.*

By the look on Mom's face, it's a safe bet that her mood hasn't improved.

"Kat, where have you been? Your father was ready to leave, but Jared insisted we find you first. Dad isn't happy with the delay."

There it is again – that familiar feeling of guilt and anger that seems to live inside me these days.

"Give me a break. I wasn't gone long."

Mom checks her watch. "Jared said it was over an hour ago when he saw you in the kitchen. Greg and Amy have been here for a while." She turns and marches to the front of the house, leaving me to glare at her retreating back.

Steph links her arm through mine. "Boy, she's in a mood."

Greg's voice echoes from the front of the house. I steer Scott and Steph through the patio door. "Let's go through the house."

Jared bursts in just as we're about to open the front door.

"Hey Kat, we've been waiting for you. Where've you been?"

Breaking away from Scott and Steph, I throw my arms around Jared's neck. "Do you really have to go?" What a stupid question. I know he has to go, but that's the first thing that pops out of my mouth.

"Yeah, I do. You'll have your turn in a few years, and then you'll understand. You'll have a blast while I'm gone. Those two over there will make sure of it." Jared pulls me off his neck and points at Scott and Steph. "Think of how quiet the house will be. You won't have to yell at me to shut up when you're trying to study."

That's true. Jared's music and friends always drive me insane when I'm trying to work.

My father's voice thunders from outside, making me cringe.

"Don't let Mom and Dad bother you. Maybe Dad'll lay off once I'm gone. I know he can be a jerk. And if he lays off, Mom'll probably relax a bit."

"I know, Jared. It's just going to be so different."

"I have to go." Jared hugs me one last time. He waves to Steph and slugs Scott on the shoulder before he opens the door.

"Oh, yeah," Jared stops and turns around. "Sarah doesn't

want to come with us now, so Greg and Amy are staying with her until you get home from work tonight."

"What? Why did she change her mind? Jared, she has to go with you."

My father shouts impatiently from outside.

"Sorry, Kat. Got to go." Jared turns and disappears through the front door.

Steph puts an arm around my shoulder. "He never changes – here one minute and gone the next."

Greg shouldn't be staying with Sarah, even with Amy around. What if he manages to get Sarah alone?

"Hello, Kat. Anybody in there?" Scott teases, knocking on my head.

"Yeah, I'm here," I answer, pushing his hands away.

"We're heading out so you can get ready for work. You okay?"

"Yeah, I'm okay. See you later. Thanks."

I watch Scott and Steph through the front window. They wave to my parents and Jared, who are pulling out of the driveway. I fight the loneliness as I turn and mope my way to my bedroom.

The house is quiet – Sarah, Greg, and Amy must still be outside. It's already weird not hearing Jared's footsteps in the house. The tears that I have been fighting all day start to fall, and I no longer try to stop them.

A glimpse of my reflection in the mirror distracts me. I never really associate myself with the girl staring back at me.

The blonde stranger looks pale, and her long hair could

use a trim, especially the bangs that will soon hang over the blue eyes. She's not really ugly or pretty – just average. She could lose a few pounds, but nobody would notice because nobody really looks close enough. She's somebody who doesn't stand out in a crowd. You'd never know how messed up she is inside.

"Are you in there, Kat?" Amy's voice on the other side of my bedroom door startles me.

"Yeah, I'm changing." My voice has a funny squeak.

"Okay. Do you want Greg to give you a ride to work?"

The panic starts to claw at me. "N-n-n-no. That's okay, I'll walk. I have lots of time."

"Are you sure? He doesn't mind."

"Yeah, I'm sure."

"Okay. We'll be outside with Sarah."

Amy's footsteps fade down the hall. The last thing I need is a ride to work with Greg. If I hurry, maybe I can sneak out of the house and not see him. I change into clean clothes and open the door.

"Shoot, I should grab a sweater," I mumble, turning around to grab the sweatshirt I threw on my dresser last night. The days are warm, but it gets cool in the evenings.

"Hello, Kat. I'd almost think you're avoiding me, but that can't be true."

I freeze, with my back to the door. How did Greg sneak down the hall without my hearing him? The ringing in my ears and pounding in my chest make me feel weak and dizzy.

The sudden touch of his hand on my shoulder makes me

drop my sweatshirt. I feel his fingers massaging my shoulder, creeping under my sleeve to stroke bare skin.

"Turn around. I'd like to see my special girl."

Chapter Three

I rush along, trying to put as much distance between Greg and me as I can. Thank goodness Sarah ran upstairs to use the bathroom when she did. Greg's hand had slid away from my shoulder when the thunder of Sarah's footsteps rang through the house.

"This isn't over," he whispered, before he strolled away. Even in the heat of the afternoon, his words chase chills through me.

The sight of the large, red hospital building brings relief. Stepping through the main entrance is like a final door slamming in Greg's face.

A little girl waves at me in the lobby. Melanie was admitted with pneumonia four days ago. Her eyes are clear now, no longer sunken, and her cheeks have a healthy flush. She lights up when she sees me.

"Hi, Kat. I'm going home!"

I crouch in front of her, smiling at her excitement. "That's great, Melly. Think of me the next time you read *Peter Rabbit*, okay?"

Melanie nods. "Okay. I'm having a birthday party. I'm going to be five. Mommy said I can have a new Peter Rabbit book." She glances at her mother. "If I'm good, right Mommy?"

"That's right, Sweetheart." Her mother rests her hand on Melanie's head and looks at me. "Thanks for spending time with her, Kat. She loved your stories. You do a wonderful job cheering up the kids while they're here."

My steps are lighter as I walk to the children's ward. My Aunt Sheila is a doctor in Pediatrics and arranged this volunteer position for me. Some kids like me to watch television with them, while others want somebody to play or read with them. The visits can be pretty tough, depending on the moods of the kids and how serious their illnesses or injuries are. Smiles like Melanie's and words of appreciation from the parents make it all worthwhile.

"Kat, you're finally here." Aunt Sheila rushes down the hall, glancing at a chart.

"Sorry. Jared got a late start. He wasn't very organized, as usual."

Aunt Sheila smiles, an absent look in her eyes. The dark, seemingly permanent circles under them are proof of many hours spent at the hospital. She even smells like the hospital, with that weird mix of stale air, medicine, antiseptics, disinfectants, and cleaning solutions that lingers in the hallways.

With an arm linked in mine, she steers me toward the nurse's station. "Kat, we had an eight-year-old girl come in through the night. She's a bit special."

"Why's that?"

"Well, her mother claims that she fell down the stairs, but I just have a weird feeling with this one. She has a broken arm. They're waiting for the swelling to go down today before they cast it, and we're waiting for some blood work results to come back. Could you spend some time with her? The mom is watching over her like a guard dog, and the girl seems agitated by her mother's presence. Just read to her, talk to her, play with her."

A page for Doctor Williams over the intercom has Aunt Sheila dashing away.

"Aunt Sheila, what's her name?" I shout at her retreating back.

"Taylor. Taylor Bradford. She's in room two fifty-six," Aunt Sheila yells over her shoulder, before disappearing into a room.

Taylor Bradford. Steph had mentioned a family named Bradford that moved to town over the summer. Mrs. Bradford works with Steph's mom at the grocery store. They also have a son, Darren, who's our age. Nobody really knows much about them, and Mrs. Bradford keeps to herself. Steph has a deep love for gossip and has made it her mission to find out more about this mysterious family. Too bad I'm bound by patient confidentiality and can't share this newest tidbit with her.

Pausing outside Taylor's partially closed door, I hear a woman talking in a hushed tone. A child whimpers at something the woman says. I knock lightly and peek in.

The little girl stares at me from the hospital bed with sad, brown eyes. Her hair falls behind her shoulders. She looks small and fragile.

"Hi Taylor, my name's Kat. I was hoping you'd like to play a game with me."

Taylor glances toward her mother. I'm sure her mother narrows her eyes at the little girl before Taylor looks back at me, eyes downcast, and shakes her head. It is impossible to misinterpret the look of disapproval on her mother's pinched face.

Normally, with this type of response, I'd leave the patient alone and move on, but Aunt Sheila seems to really want me to spend time with Taylor. Feeling nervous, I step into the room and head to the corner cupboard where the books are kept. The familiar, musty smell of books and crayons in the cupboard calms me with its promise of escape into other worlds that only books can provide.

Grabbing the book on the top of the pile, I take a deep breath and turn to face Taylor and her mother. "How about we read a story, Taylor? I used to love Peter Rabbit when I was your age."

"I think Taylor needs to sleep right now," her mother says. She's perched in a chair beside the bed, as if guarding Taylor from something.

Defeated, I decide not to push the situation any further, until Taylor looks at me with sad, pleading eyes. There's something about her expression that makes me want to help her.

"I'm sure you're right, Mrs. Bradford," I say, more determined than ever. "I always loved a great bedtime story before going to sleep. What do you think, Taylor? Would a story help you go to sleep?"

Taylor smiles shyly when I approach the bed so I can sit down beside her. I'm close enough to see the ugly blue and purple bruise on her cheek and the gash on her forehead. Her right arm is in a sling against her chest. The sleeve of her hospital gown has slid up to reveal another bruise, the size of my fist, on her left arm. I suspect there are more bruises on her legs, hidden under the white sheets.

"I'm going to sit on the bed with you, Taylor. You let me know if it hurts when the mattress shifts with my weight. Okay?"

Taylor nods. She winces once as I position myself on the bed, but never says a word.

"I don't think this is a good time. Taylor really needs to sleep right now." Mrs. Bradford fidgets with the blanket on the bed and glances toward the door. She isn't as sour when her lips aren't pinched in disapproval. She almost looks afraid of something or someone. I can understand why my aunt has a funny feeling about something not being right.

"Mommy, please—" Taylor's plea is cut off as Aunt Sheila enters the room.

"Mrs. Bradford, would you come with me for a minute? I'd like to speak to you about Taylor's care and medication before she leaves to have her cast put on."

"Why can't you speak to me here?" Mrs. Bradford asks.

"It's best we have a bit of privacy while Kat entertains your daughter with stories. Kat always does such a wonderful job with the children."

Mrs. Bradford casts a reluctant look toward her daughter. It's obvious she doesn't want to leave me alone with her. "Taylor, I'll be right back," she says. The words are forceful and seem to carry hidden messages.

Mrs. Bradford rises from the chair and glances back at us. Aunt Sheila uses the opportunity to wink at me before she escorts Taylor's mom out the door. Thank goodness for Aunt Sheila.

"Okay, Taylor. Let's read this story. Do you like Peter Rabbit?"

The little girl shrugs. "I don't know. I don't read many books."

"Books are full of magical stories. I have a little sister about your age and she loves it when I read to her."

Taylor looks surprised. "You read to your sister?"

I nod. "Of course. Sometimes we do other things. We play or watch a movie together, but my favorite thing is reading a book." *Well, we used to do those things together, but not as much lately.*

"I wish I had a big sister. I bet that's better than having a brother." Taylor looks down at the bed sheets.

"Oh, I don't know. I have a big brother and we have lots of fun together."

Taylor is quiet for a moment before she whispers, "I think a sister would be better." She looks back up at me. "Could you read to me like you do to your sister? I could pretend we're sisters."

Suddenly I want to hug Taylor and never let go. I've just met her, yet I feel so many different emotions – sympathy, sorrow, protectiveness, and a strange connection I can't explain. She continues staring at me with the only sign of hope in her eyes that I've seen since entering the room.

"That's a great idea. Let's get started."

While I read the story to Taylor, she slips her hand onto my lap. When she awards me with her first smile and asks for another book, I'm all hers.

"Sure. Let's see what's here." Rummaging in the cupboard, I talk to Taylor, hoping she'll confide in me. "Does your arm hurt very much, Taylor?"

"When I move, it does."

"Did you fall? Is that how you hurt yourself?"

Taylor looks away from me. "Down the stairs," she whispers.

"Ouch. Once I slipped on something on the stairs and fell. Is that what happened to you?"

Still looking toward the wall, Taylor shakes her head. "No, I just fell."

Taylor's fingers on her free hand twist in the blanket.

Instinct tells me not to push her too hard. "Okay, I found another book."

By the time Mrs. Bradford rushes back into the room, we're on our fourth book. Taylor has actually giggled at the silliness of a Dr. Seuss story. Her hand is now resting comfortably on my lap and she's no longer fidgeting with the blanket.

"Okay Taylor, it's time for you to take a nap. We're going to go for your cast shortly." Mrs. Bradford sounds slightly breathless. She looks at me. "I'm sure other children would love to hear one of your stories."

Tears gather in Taylor's eyes. "But Mommy, I'm not tired. I want to hear more stories."

Mrs. Bradford's voice becomes sharp and agitated. "I'll read you a story, Taylor. Kat has other little boys and girls to visit now."

Taylor looks at me. "Do you really have to go, Kat?"

Mrs. Bradford cuts off my reply. "Taylor, don't question me."

Not wanting to cause more trouble for the poor little girl, I squeeze her hand. "Your Mommy's right. I have to go see the other kids. I had so much fun with you that I forgot all about them."

Tears slide down Taylor's cheeks. "Okay, I guess." Taylor glances at her mother and then back at me. "Will it hurt when they fix my arm?"

I smile at her. "No, it won't hurt. Your friends will be able to sign their name and draw on your cast when you get home."

The little girl frowns. "My friends can't come to my house."

"Taylor, that's enough," her mother cuts in. "It's time for Kat to go."

With a final squeeze of Taylor's hand, I rise from the bed. At the door, I turn to say good-bye. She looks even sadder than she did when I entered the room. All the smiles are gone.

Taylor, I know exactly how you feel. I promise you are not alone.

The knot in my stomach throbs with a life of its own while I walk down the hall, reminding me that I, too, am not alone.

Chapter Four

"Sit up straight, Kat. You'll be a hunchback by the time you're thirty."

I snort in response. "I'm not one of your precious students, Mom."

"That's enough," Dad cuts in. "Can't we finish breakfast in peace? I know it's the first day of school and everybody's on edge, but I don't want to listen to this."

"Sorry, David. I'm just anxious about taking on my new class and the new principal." Mom shuffles papers together and puts them into her briefcase. Here we go again. Dad snaps a command and Mom begs for forgiveness.

Dad turns to me. "Kat, what time is your last class? I need you home with Sarah. I have an important meeting at four o'clock that I can't miss and your mother will be late tonight."

"Dad, I'm working after school. My schedule has been up on the fridge for a week."

"Your mom will give Sheila a call. She'll understand if you can't make it." Dad glances at Mom and she nods her head like a well-trained puppy.

"No, don't call Aunt Sheila. I'm not staying home to watch Sarah. I'm not your live-in babysitter."

"Kat, please," Mom interrupts, trying to be the peace-keeper. "Sarah's already caught her bus, so it's too late to make arrangements for her to go to a friend's. Maybe Amy can come over later. I'm not sure if she's working at the bank today or not."

"Great idea, Maria. Call her." Dad sets down his news-paper and sips his coffee, while Mom walks away to call Amy.

"Yes, *sir*," I mumble.

"What was that?" Dad snaps. "Why do you have to mouth back all the time? We never got half the lip from Jared that we get from you. Even Sarah is better behaved."

I roll my eyes. Great way to start the school year – listen-ing to one of Dad's lectures about why I can't be more like Jared or a little princess like precious Sarah. I hate the way he barks his commands and tries to control every situation. Sometimes he reminds me so much of Greg that it's eerie. They played football in high school, went to university together, and now they're partners in their own law firm.

Mom comes back to the table and sits down. "Amy said she isn't working today, so she can come over to stay with Sarah. I don't know what we'd do without her and Greg."

Dad grunts and buries his nose in the newspaper again.

"It's a shame they couldn't have children." Mom pours milk into her coffee and looks at me. "They've always been so wonderful with you kids. They love children."

I choke on my milk. It gushes from my mouth, into my cereal, and onto the table. *Did I hear her right?*

"For Pete's sake, Kat, what's wrong with you today?" Mom demands. She gets up from the table and throws the dishcloth at me. Dad glances up from his newspaper, annoyance flickering across his stern features while I cough.

Like a fool, I sputter, "Love children? I'll say he loves children – he loves them a little too much! You should be grateful he doesn't have kids of his own."

"I don't want to hear another word from you this morning. I've had enough." Dad slaps down his paper and stands up, his eyes narrowing.

"Fine!" I throw the dishcloth on the table, and stomp across the kitchen to my knapsack. "And don't worry…I'll have a great day. Thanks for your concern. Better yet, thanks for nothing!"

Fighting to hold back the tears, I march down our long, winding driveway to catch the school bus.

Steph and Scott are already standing at the side of the road. They live across from us, so we always catch the bus together. I try to compose myself before they see me.

"Gads, girl, couldn't you have found a new outfit to wear for our first day?" Steph yells, shaking her head in obvious disgust.

Can't anybody give me a break today? I shrug. "At least I'm comfortable."

I eye Steph's skin-tight white pants and fancy sandals. I would be limping by the end of the day in those shoes and wouldn't be able to breathe in the pants.

"The guys'll never notice you dressed like that. I could probably fit into that shirt with you!"

I shrug again. This is my favorite red T-shirt and I like my baggy, cut-off jeans. Attracting attention from the guys at school is the last thing on my mind. Actually, I'd prefer that they just leave me alone.

"Lay off, Steph," Scott interrupts. "She looks fine."

Steph glares at her brother. "What do you know?"

"I know lots. Just because—"

I cut in to stop the arguing. "Okay, you guys. Let's talk about something else. I've already had enough fighting for the day with my parents."

Scott grimaces and Steph pouts. She hates not having the last word in any discussion. Before she can say anything else, I tell them about Taylor and my Aunt's suspicions. I'm careful not to mention any names so that I don't breach my patient confidentiality agreement.

"No way," says Steph, obviously taken with this newest bit of gossip. I can picture the wheels spinning in her head as she tries to figure out who the family could be.

"Oh, guess who's the new principal at your mom's school," Steph says, changing the subject.

Shrugging, I try to remember if Mom has mentioned a name.

Grinning, Steph announces, "It's that new guy in town, Mr. Bradford. Mom finally managed to get that bit of information at work the other day from his weird wife. Mom said they're calling her Mrs. Clamford because when anybody tries to talk to her, she clams right up."

My heart drops to my stomach. How could Mr. Bradford be a principal and be beating up his own kid? Would he do that to other kids at school? Maybe Aunt Sheila's funny feeling is wrong this time.

"Hey, do you think principals have to go through some kind of screening process to make sure they're all right around kids?" I ask.

"Don't know," Scott says, looking down the road.

"What if a principal abuses kids?" I ask, unwilling to let the subject drop.

"Gads, I'd hope he doesn't hurt kids if he's a principal," Steph says.

Hearing Steph say *Gads* takes me back. When we were seven or eight years old, we made up the word to bug Scott and Jared. They could never figure out what it meant because we had different meanings for it all the time. Our favorites were "Guys Are Disgusting Snakes" and "Girls Are Dreadfully Smart." Later it just became our way of saying "Gosh Almighty,

Do be Serious." Silly as it is, we have stuck to using it over the years.

"How could that happen?" Scott asks, bringing my thoughts back to the present. "How could a guy hide something like that if he worked with kids all the time? People would know and the kids would tell."

"Yeah, for once I guess you're right." Steph shrugs.

I'm suddenly angry. How can people be so naïve? Do they think jerks who like to hurt kids walk around with a neon sign on their foreheads or something? Do they think it's easy for kids to come forward and tell the truth?

"Don't be so sure," I snap, unable to suppress my anger. "You'd be surprised how much people can hide. You never know someone as well as you think."

The bus pulls up. I walk past Scott and Steph and climb into the bus. The three of us are quiet during the ride to school.

Chapter Five

The day just keeps getting worse. I have Ms. Jackson for English. She loves to assign last-minute essays on a Friday afternoon. Steph and I have separate lunch periods. My schedule lists a French history class I never registered for. To top things off, it seems the whole perky cheerleading squad is in my science class. Listening to them gush about tryouts and boys and breaking nails makes me feel like a freak because I couldn't care less about such things.

The only bright spot is that I'm on my way to work and hope to see Taylor again.

When I see the loneliness and fear in Taylor's eyes, I feel like I'm looking into a mirror. We seem to share a secret that keeps us separate from normal people. *Do I want to help her because I can't help myself?*

On my way through the lobby, I think about my conversation with Scott and Steph. How could a man like Mr. Bradford get a job as a principal? How do people like him and Greg fool everybody?

I caught a glimpse of Taylor's brother, Darren, at school today. Darren and Taylor look nothing alike. He's tall and blond. Taylor is small and fragile-looking, with brown hair. From what I saw and heard from other people, Darren seems to be a loner.

"Hi, Kat, how was school today?" I look up, realizing I'm already at the nurses' station. I smile at Wanda, the nurse on duty.

"Not so great, Wanda. Is Dr. Williams around?"

Wanda nods. "She's here somewhere. She's been here since she was called in at three this morning. I don't know how she stays on her feet by the end of the day. If anything ever happened to one of my babies, I'd want her looking after them, for sure."

"Yeah, she's a great doctor. How's Taylor doing today? Did everything go okay with her cast?"

Wanda's smile evaporates. She motions me back into the empty office behind the nurses' station. "She went home. Dr. Williams tried to keep her here, but Mrs. Bradford insisted on Taylor's release. She said Taylor didn't need to stay any longer."

"Isn't there anything we can do?" I feel sick at the thought of Taylor being hurt again. Wanda was the nurse looking after Taylor, so I knew we could talk about the situation.

"Not really, Kat. Dr. Williams called and reported her

suspicions. Their situation will be looked into, but if Taylor won't talk, there isn't much that can be done."

"That sucks."

Wanda nods. "We see it around here more than you might think, but so many of the kids are too scared to say anything." Wanda sighs and looks at the patient registry in her hand.

"We had a few new children admitted last night. You could start with them and work your way around to the others that are still here."

"Thanks, Wanda." A heavy, hopeless feeling lodges in my chest. *Why won't Taylor tell us what's happening to her? Can't she see things would get better if she would tell us the truth? He would never be able to hurt her again. Get serious! I can't even bring myself to tell the truth about Greg. I'm as guilty as Taylor for letting him touch me and get away with it.*

Amy is still at the house with Sarah when I get home from work. Working with the kids at the hospital has made me feel better. Then Amy mentions calling Greg to come pick her up.

"I'm sure Mom or Dad will give you a ride home when they get here."

"That's okay, Kat. Greg dropped me off on his way to see a client. He won't mind coming back this way. He loves to see you and Sarah."

"Where is Sarah?"

"She's in her room. She wanted to draw a picture of a princess for Greg. She's such a sweet little thing." Amy picks up the phone and starts to dial.

I head to Sarah's room to see how her first day of school went. "Hey, Squirt, how was school?"

Sarah looks up from her paper and markers. "Great. I got Mrs. Finch. She's the best third grade teacher in the whole school. Dory and Kaly are in my class, too."

"That's great, Sarah."

"What about you?"

I stick my tongue out and make a face, scrunching up my nose and crossing my eyes. "Not so great."

Sarah giggles, making me feel better than I have all day. Dropping on the bed beside her, I start to tickle her. We roll around, wrestling and tickling each other until we hear the front door open and a deep, male voice.

Sarah jumps off the bed. "Greg's here!" She runs out of the room before I can stop her.

Taking a deep breath, I brace myself for the sight of Greg. I just have to stay away from him so he can't touch me. *Just keep my distance and don't end up alone with him.*

What I see when I enter the kitchen makes me want to run to the bathroom and throw up. Sarah has jumped up into Greg's arms to give him a hug and has her legs wrapped around him. His arms and slimy hands are squeezing her, and Amy is standing there, smiling, as if everything is fine.

"Sarah, get down right now." My voice sounds distant and strange to my ears. I'm vaguely aware of Amy staring at me oddly, but my focus remains on Sarah, who is still in Greg's arms.

"Sarah, get down," I repeat.

Sarah turns and glares at me. I release the breath I'm holding when her feet touch the floor, and she moves away from Greg. She stops in front of me and shakes her finger. "You're not the boss. You can't tell me what to do. I'm telling Daddy when he gets home." She runs down the hall. The slam of her bedroom door echoes through the house.

"Kat, that was uncalled for," Amy says, staring at me with a surprised expression.

Greg's eyes narrow, like a predator ready to pounce on his victim. It's the same look he has when I tell him I don't want him to touch me. His eyes always gleam smugly with the knowledge that he's bigger and stronger, leaving me with no choice. He seems to grow taller as he stands there, his shadow swallowing me, leaving me helpless.

His expression changes within a split second when Amy turns around to look at him. Breathing heavily, I back up a few steps, trying to put more distance between us.

"What's with you two?" Amy looks back and forth between us.

Greg shrugs. "You have a tough day at school, Kiddo?" He looks at me with a smug, can't-beat-me smile. I deflate like a balloon, all of my strength disappearing. He's right. I can't beat him.

"Guess so," I mumble and look at Amy. "Thanks for watching Sarah, Amy. See you around." I purposely avoid looking at Greg and walk to my bedroom, forcing myself not to run like the terrified victim he's created.

I sit on my bed and stare out the window at the blue sky,

waiting for the sound of the front door to close behind them. Feeling lost and frightened sucks. I hate it. I don't want to feel like this anymore.

I used to convince myself it was all a dream. When he touched me and made me lie on this very bed, I could often push it from my mind as if it wasn't happening. When the creepy feeling of his hands on my skin bothered me, I'd tell myself that it was okay because I was his special girl, and he loved me. I often wondered why I wasn't special to my father. Why didn't he ever say nice things like Greg did?

When did I start feeling more uncomfortable and realize that what Greg was doing and saying to me was wrong? When did I start avoiding him? The last few years, I've struggled with acknowledging what is truly happening and what to do. I hate myself for not being able to stop him.

"Kat, are you in there?" Startled at the sound of my mother's voice, I nod stupidly as if she can see me through the closed door.

"Kat?" my mother repeats.

"Yeah, I'm here."

My mom walks in, still in her brand-new back-to-school skirt and jacket. She has to be the best-dressed teacher I've ever seen. Most teachers I know dress casually, but I don't remember ever seeing Mom leave for work in a pair of pants.

The mattress shifts as she sits beside me. Tracing the swirling pattern on my comforter with my finger, I remember the scene from this morning. Scenes like that have been occurring more frequently between my parents and me, especially with my father. When Jared is around, he buffers the arguments, but he's not here now.

I'm so angry and frustrated with them sometimes. At other times I regret every horrible thing I've said and wish they'd hold me close, like they did when I was little.

"How was school, Kat?"

"Okay." It's easier to just tell her what she wants to hear.

"Great."

An awkward silence falls between us.

Sighing, I realize Mom is providing me with the opening to smooth things over after this morning's argument. After the confrontation about Greg, I want to curl up on her lap, like I did as a kid. As if sensing my mood, she reaches over and puts her arm around me. Her warmth chases some of the chill from my heart. I'm safe for the moment.

"How was school for you?" I ask her, realizing that I really do care about her day. "How was the new principal?"

"Better than I thought. The principal is nice, and so far my class is behaving. But I can already tell that I have a few troublemakers."

Curious after my conversation with Steph and Scott, I decide to find out more.

"Is the principal the new guy in town – Mr. Bradford?"

"Yeah. Do you know him?"

I shake my head, trying to figure out how to say something without intruding on Taylor's privacy. "I met his daughter. His wife seems kind of weird."

"He asked about my family. When I told him you volunteer

at the hospital, he mentioned his little girl was hospitalized after a bad fall. Is that where you met her? Tyler, isn't it?"

"Taylor. And yeah, she was there when I was working."

We're both silent for a moment. I want to find out more, without giving my aunt's suspicions and actions away.

"Mom, I heard some funny rumors about their family at school." I cross my fingers behind my back for the little white lie I'm telling. "Do you think it's possible for him to be hurting his daughter?"

"Hogwash. He's a nice man and he was very concerned about his little girl. People around here thrive on gossip, especially when it has to do with newcomers or strangers in town."

"Kat!" Dad bellows from the kitchen. It doesn't sound like he came home happy.

Flinching, I mumble, "I just can't please him, anymore."

"Now Kat, that's not true. Dad's just under a lot of pressure at work and he misses Jared."

I jump off the bed and run out of the room when he shouts my name for the second time. The longer he's kept waiting, the worse it'll be.

Sarah, with red, swollen eyes, is standing beside Dad. His arm is draped cozily over her shoulder. *The little tattletale!* Squaring my shoulders, I look into his eyes and wait for the fireworks to start.

I don't have to wait long.

"What's wrong with you? Greg and Amy are our friends. Why would you yell at Sarah for hugging Greg and tell her to get away?" I open my mouth to speak, but Dad isn't finished yet.

38

"That's not how we treat friends in this house. That's not how you treat your sister, either. If you're going to come home with an attitude every night, you can just march that attitude right to your room and stay there."

I'm prevented from answering once again as Dad continues his tirade.

"I don't know where we've gone wrong with you, Katrine. We've never had these problems with your brother. Greg is right about teenage girls."

The why-can't-you-be-like-your-brother speech is something I don't feel the need to hear again, especially after hearing Dad referring to Greg being right about anything related to teenage girls – me in particular. I turn and storm toward my room.

"Katrine, come back here. Do *not* turn your back on me!"

Mom appears, like a guardian angel swooping down to save me. She pats me on the shoulder and motions with her eyes for me to keep going. It's been a while since she's stepped in to help me with Dad.

Mom's soft but firm voice follows me down the hall. "David, she's had enough. Why don't we…" I close my bedroom door, blocking the voices in the kitchen.

Jared. My father compares everything I do to Jared. I used to be jealous when Dad would compare me to my brother. Strangely enough, it's Jared who helped me through that. His jokes and imitations of Dad would eventually bring a small smile to my face, no matter how upset Dad had made me. In no time at all, Jared would have me rolling on my bed, clutching my sides and laughing until I ran to the bathroom to pee. Jared doesn't like being Dad's pet, and this was his way of making it up to me. He tried telling Dad to lay off once, but that didn't go well.

Missing my brother, I reach for my phone and dial his number. One little joke from him could help me forget this whole rotten day.

"Hello?" A strange voice answers.

"Hi, is Jared there?"

"Who?"

"Jared. Jared Thompson."

"Hold on." I flinch when the guy at the other end yells for Jared. The least he could do is cover the receiver.

"Nope. He's not around."

A girl giggles in the background and somebody turns the music up louder.

"Could you ask him to call Kat?"

"Sure, Nat. No problem." The dial tone sounds before I can correct him.

It's doubtful that Jared will get his message.

Chapter Six

Friday, September 8.

This week sucks. True, it did get better after that horrible first day of school. It still sucks, though. I'm glad it's Friday!

I dropped that stupid French history class. The guidance counsellor swears I signed up for it and I swear I didn't. I signed up for creative writing instead. That should be cool.

They changed my schedule around for the writing class so now I have lunch period with Steph and Scott again. I'm starting to think that isn't so great. All Steph wants to do is talk about guys. I don't know what she sees in them - they're nothing but trouble. I'm sick of acting interested in her chatter. Her latest crush is some guy named Mike, who hangs out with a bunch of thugs. Talk about jerk alert! She sits in the cafeteria staring at him with her lame, puppy eyes.

Steph and I have always been able to talk about anything until lately. All she talks about now is boys, fancy clothes, and makeup. It bugs me that I'm feeling this way. She's been my best friend forever.

Scott seems to avoid us a lot. He sometimes sits with a few other guys from his biology class. I caught him looking at me kind of funny a few times. I don't know what's up with him. He's different lately, as if he's uncomfortable being around us sometimes. He is often irritable and snaps at us. I miss the way things used to be.

What's happening to me? Things keep changing that shouldn't. I don't understand why good things change, but bad things never go away.

No word on Taylor. She just dropped off the face of the earth. I hope she's okay. I just wish somebody could help her. Everybody seems to think Mr. Bradford is so great. Everybody seems to think Greg is so great too, and I'm the only one who knows that's not true.

No word from Jared. Who knows if he even got my message? I tried again last night, but nobody picked up. He's disappeared too.

It's too bad Greg won't disappear that easily!

"Kat, are you out here?" Mom yells from the backyard.

I glance at my watch and realize it's getting late. Stretching, I try to work the stiffness out of my muscles. I've been sitting scrunched up at the small table in the clubhouse too long.

Mom and Amy must be ready to go. They're doing a girl's night out – dinner and a show. Mom is already stressed over her class at school, so Amy has made it her mission to calm her down. That's something Dad has never been very good at.

If anybody were to ask me, which will never happen, I'd say that Mom is more stressed about not hearing from Jared. Dad asks every night at the supper table if anybody has heard from his "University Boy." Mom fidgets, says no, and mentions she's worried. Dad shrugs it off and says that he must be having fun.

Carefully replacing my journal behind the milk crates, I leave the clubhouse. Mom is standing at the back door of our house, the cordless phone in her hand.

"Steph wants to talk to you," she says, giving me the phone.

"Thanks." I walk back to the wooden swing that hangs from an old oak tree along the edge of our backyard. It's been there since I turned three. The bright red paint peeled off long ago. The wood is gray and weathered from the sun.

Dangling my legs and swaying back and forth on the swing, I turn off the hold button.

"Hey, what's up?" I ask.

"Why aren't you answering your cell? Forget it. Guess what!"

No "hi" or "how are you" or anything. Just a breathless "guess what." It must have something to do with Mike.

"Hi to you too," I reply.

"Come on Kat, I don't have much time."

"I give, Steph. What?"

"You'll never guess who called. Go ahead, guess."

For somebody who doesn't have much time, Steph is being pretty dramatic. Trying to put as much enthusiasm into my voice as possible, I make my guess. "Mike?"

Steph squeals so loud on the other end, I have to hold the phone away from my ear.

"He asked me out, Kat. Can you believe it? Maybe he caught those vibes I was sending him in the cafeteria all week."

"I doubt it. I think he just has a thing for puppy dogs and noticed your sappy stare." I struggle to hide my sarcasm, trying to keep my voice light and teasing.

Steph giggles. "Whatever, it doesn't matter. He called. I felt so stupid. I didn't know what to say to him on the phone. But he still asked me out."

I can see Steph doing a happy dance around her bedroom. "That's great," I reply, trying to be happy for her.

"I couldn't believe it when he asked me what I'm doing tonight. He wants to go to that party we heard about all week. It'll mainly be seniors."

The familiar burning in the back of my throat keeps me from replying at first. Steph knows this week has been dif-ficult for me, and she promised to come over tonight for a movie and sleepover. I've been looking forward to it and had even hoped it would help some of the strain I've been feeling between us lately.

"Kat, are you still there?"

"Yeah." My voice sounds croaky.

"Kat, I'm sorry. I know I promised to come over but—"

"It's okay, Steph." I cut her off before we both feel awkward over her cancelling. "You go ahead. Have fun tonight. I'm kind of beat, anyway. I'd probably be a drag and fall asleep early."

Steph's laugh sounds forced. "You're the best, Kat. Why don't you come to the party? Mike knows a lot of people who will be there. I could use your company. I won't know anybody."

The thought of tagging along on Steph's date to a house full of drunken seniors doesn't sound appealing.

"Nope, count me out. I'm turning in early."

"Are you sure?" She doesn't even wait for my answer before continuing. "I better go. I have to find something to wear."

"Yeah, you wouldn't want my help there," I reply, trying to break the ice.

Steph laughs and hangs up.

The dial tone drones in my ear, while I sway gently on the swing. Just like that she's gone, and I'm spending Friday night alone. Not feeling up to spending the evening with Dad or Sarah, I put the phone in my pocket and walk past the clubhouse to the river.

The breeze carries the smell of diesel fuel from the Thomas farm on the other side of the woods. A squirrel scampers by me with a cheek full of nuts and who knows what else for its winter collection. I step to the side to stay out of its path, careful to avoid any patches of poison ivy. Jared and I learned about poison ivy the hard way one summer.

The smell of wet moss greets me as I emerge from the trees and stop on the riverbank, careful not to slip on the rocks. Sometimes, when the water level is low and it hasn't rained for awhile, you can see to the river bottom where the carp sunbathe. The water is dark and murky today, hiding any fish that may be watching me below the surface.

Thinking of Steph again, I throw a stone sideways and watch it skip across the water. The skips match the rhythm of the words that repeat in my head. *I can't believe she did that.* She just dropped me for some guy. Some best friend she is. So much for loyalty and all that crap. One stupid phone call and some guy she barely knows is more important to her than me. Why did I let her off the hook so easy? Why didn't I tell her how hurt I feel? Before I know it I'm crying.

Because I don't deserve any better.

The river is quiet. The ripples from the stone spread across the water and disappear, as if they never existed. The stone is gone, swallowed up, never to be seen again. My arm is suspended in the air, another stone held tightly between my fingers.

What if I just disappeared like that? Would anybody care?

The river water becomes darker, and my head spins. The pictures come fast and furious. Greg is standing over me, pulling his zipper up. I'm seven years old again, staring at him with a mixture of fear and blind adoration.

"You're a very special girl. Nobody else loves you the way I do. You understand that, don't you?"

I nod, believing every word. He loves me. He wouldn't lie.

"That's my Kitty Kat." Greg rubs my cheek with his hand. "You can't trust anyone like you can me – especially your daddy. He'll be angry and think you're bad if he finds out about our special love. He wouldn't want you anymore."

My naïve heart breaks at Greg's words. My world is shattered by the perceived betrayal of my father.

The picture of Greg fades when the stone falls out of my hand with a sudden plop. I try to climb back into the present. I shiver at how real the scene felt and turn, half expecting to see Greg standing there beside me.

"Get a grip," I whisper, in an effort to shake off the eerie feeling. It's like being haunted by myself as a child. The memories flood back and trap me when I least expect them.

Even after Greg told me so many times when I was growing up that no one would like me if I told, I never really believed I could lose Jared or Steph. I've always been able to depend on them, but lately they haven't been there for me.

You're weak and worthless.

Staring at the water where the last stone sank to the bottom, I wonder why I'm here. Why was I put on this earth? The only one who seems to care about me is Greg. *Could it be that I was put here for Greg? No! What he's doing to me can't be right.*

I launch another stone with all the force I can muster. The

plop it makes, breaking through the water and sinking to the bottom, is gratifying. I had complete control over the stone before throwing it and it felt good. If only I had some control over my own life.

A twig snapping behind me breaks into my thoughts. Spinning around, I look into Steph's face.

"Hey," she says, a bit sheepishly, lowering her eyes to look at the ground.

"Don't you have a hot and heavy date?" I reply, failing to hide the sarcasm in my voice. She's wearing a short, tight skirt and shirt. Every hair on her head is neatly arranged and cemented with hair spray so it won't move.

Steph shrugs and looks up at me. "Yeah, I do."

My hands fidget, but I don't try to stop them. *Let her see that I'm upset.*

"I was hoping you'd change your mind. I'd really like you to come to the party. It wouldn't be any fun without you."

I start to thaw. Does she still need me? Then I recall our phone conversation and how quickly she ditched me for Mike, and the warm feeling fades.

"I don't think so, Steph. It's not my thing." I turn back to the river, pick up another stone and throw it, watching it skip across the surface before joining its friends on the bottom.

"Please, Kat. I'm…well, I'm nervous and scared."

I skip another stone.

"You always were great at that," she says.

The corners of my mouth tilt slightly. I couldn't hit a base-ball to save my life, and I fell all over the soccer field when Jared and Scott tried to teach me to play. Give me a stone, though, and I could beat them all. Jared, Scott, and even Steph would practice by the hour to beat my record of eighteen skips, but none of them ever came close.

The grass rustles behind me and Steph's voice seems closer. "Please, Kat. You're my best friend. I need you."

Gads. I needed to hear those words. The sweet sound of them softens my resolve to avoid the party.

"Besides," Steph continues, "I'm sure you don't want to watch hockey with your dad and Greg tonight."

Confused, I turn to face Steph. "What'd you say? Greg's here?"

"Yeah, your mom and Amy were leaving when I walked over. Greg and your dad are here with Sarah, watching hockey. A night of male testosterone – yuck! Poor Sarah."

I should have known Greg would come with Amy. My desire to avoid him is far stronger than my dislike of going to the party.

"I suppose somebody has to make sure you behave," I say, shrugging and turning away from the river.

How bad could the party be?

Chapter Seven

I haven't seen Steph for at least an hour. I scan the smoky room from my spot on the couch, but still don't see her. *Where are you? I don't want to fight my way through this mob by myself. Please come tell me you hate it here and want to go home.*

My view is blocked by a large butt that has stopped in front of me. Seeing past the cheeky mass is impossible. It sways every time I try to peek around it. I swear if I ever get out of here, I'll never speak to Steph again.

The guy beside me pokes his elbow into my ribs for the fifth time, while he wrestles with his buddy. If I don't get some fresh air soon, I'll burst. A bead of sweat trickles between my shoulder blades. After a few more minutes of Dodge-That-Butt, I poke it in frustration.

No reaction. I poke again. "Hey, Butt Boy!" No response, but the blonde sitting on the arm of the couch giggles like an idiot.

Glaring at the blonde, I get ready for a harder poke. Before I make contact, the butt falls toward me. With nowhere to escape on the crowded couch, I push myself as far back into the cushion as I can, before it crashes down.

The impact of the landing pushes us both deep into the couch. Butt Boy falls across my lap, into the guy beside me, spilling his drink on the carpet and my white running shoes. The guy beside me loses his drink and it spills down the side of my yellow shirt.

I'm not going to cry. I'm not going to let these people see me break down. I blink against the blur of tears, silently willing them to go away before anybody notices. *Please let me wake up from this nightmare.*

I spot Steph, who's being dragged across the room by Mike. *Thank you! Finally, we can leave.*

"See? I told you not to worry," Mike shouts at Steph. "She's found her own friend." He pulls Steph out of the room. She looks over her shoulder and mouths that she's sorry before disappearing.

With a sinking heart, I watch her go, leaving me alone in a room full of drunken strangers, with the largest one sprawled across my lap. How could she do this to me? I look away, wiping a tear off my cheek.

"Ah, don't cry, Babe. I love you," slurs Butt Boy.

Something snaps inside me. The shouts and loud music

recede to a dull hum as I focus on my one and only goal – to find the front door and leave this awful place.

With a mighty heave, I push the drunk off my lap and onto the floor. "Get off me, Bubble Butt."

I barge my way through the crowd, searching for Steph. Fingers dig into my arms and steady me when I stumble over some garbage. I look into the eyes of my rescuer and attempt to thank him. He cuts me off. "You look like you could use some strong hands tonight, Baby."

"In your dreams," I shout and continue pushing my way through the crowd.

The cigarette smoke burns my throat and my lungs are begging for unpolluted air. My shoes stick to the floor with every step. *I should just leave Steph here. Why am I looking for her? She abandoned me. She doesn't need me, so I don't need her.*

Finally, I make it into the kitchen. An elbow digs into my breast and I'm shoved from behind. That's it. I need out.

I glance around. There's a base for a cordless phone hanging on the wall, but no phone.

"Anybody know where the phone is?" I shout over the din. Nobody answers.

"Forget it," I mumble and push my way to the front door.

Outside, the house behind me pulses with life while I greedily suck in the fresh air.

What now? It's a long, cool walk home. Why didn't I grab my cell phone before I came? *I didn't grab it because it was in the family room and I didn't want to see Greg. The guy is making me afraid of going into my own house.*

I shiver when a breeze blows my wet shirt against me. I can't stand out here all night.

We passed a convenience store on the way here in Mike's car. Maybe they have a phone I could use.

The lights of the convenience store light up the night. A car pulls out of the parking lot and somebody shouts, "Hey, Beautiful, want to go for a ride?" Hoots and hollers come from inside the car and fade away as it turns the corner.

There's an old pay phone at the side of the building. I dig into my pocket for a quarter, relieved to find one. At least something has gone right tonight.

Who should I call? I can't call home with Greg there. He'd either come for me, or Dad would leave him alone with Sarah. The thought of either scenario makes me cringe.

Scott – of course! I'll call Scott. Please be home, I silently beg while dialling the phone.

"Hello?"

"Scott?" My voice sounds choked and breathless.

"Kat?"

"Yeah, it's me. Can you come get me? Steph dragged me to this party, and now I'm stuck."

"What party? The one they've been talking about at school?"

"Yeah, that one. Can you come?"

"What were you thinking going there? Forget it. I'm not coming out there."

"Please, Scott. I don't want to call my dad and I just need to get out of here."

After a pause that feels like an eternity, Scott says he'll be there in a few minutes.

I tell him where to find me and walk into the store to wait. The cashier glances suspiciously at me while I stand just inside the door. Finally, Scott pulls up in his mom's van and I slip into the passenger seat. "Thanks, Scott. I wanted out of there so bad."

"Where's Steph?"

"She's still there with Mike." I turn toward the side window, unable to stand the look of disappointment on Scott's face.

"You mean Mike Turner?" Scott asks.

"Yeah, that's him. She's been mooning over him all week."

"He's bad news. What's she doing with him?"

I turn toward Scott, annoyed. "How should I know? She was fine when I left."

"Why would you let her be with him? That crowd only wants to party, drink, and smoke up."

I lean back against the headrest, trying to ignore Scott's lecture. My whole body feels tired. My muscles no longer want to function and I can almost feel myself floating when I close my eyes.

The van rolls forward to pull out of the parking lot.

"Are you sure she's okay?" Scott's tone has changed, as if he's finally clued in to my mood.

I look over at him and nod. "She's a big girl, Scott. She's fine. She wants to be there." He's obviously concerned for his sister.

Scott stops the van at a red light and glances at me. "At least one of you had enough brains to leave before things got out of control." My eyes fall shut again. "You okay? You look beat."

"Yeah, it's been a rough week. I could sleep for two days straight."

"I'm sorry. I guess I haven't been around much. I should've been there for you more with Jared leaving and everything."

"Yeah, Jared leaving, my parents—" *Greg.*

"Anything I can do?"

He looks so sincere and concerned. None of his earlier annoyance is showing now.

I shake my head and whisper, "Just be my friend." For the first time in a while, I feel safe and warm.

A comfortable silence wraps around us. The night feels peaceful. My muscles relax and I sink into the van's seat. Closing my eyes, my mind lets go, and I drift off to sleep.

"Hey, we're home." Scott's hand presses into my shoulder. Surfacing, I see Scott's dark, chocolate-colored eyes staring at me. He's always had the kindest, warmest eyes. Never once have they turned cold and calculating like Greg's.

Why does Greg always have to pop into my head? Why does everything come back to him?

Awkwardly jerking the van door open, I turn to thank Scott. I pause when he puts his hand on my arm.

"What just freaked you out?" Scott sounds so sincere, like he really cares and wants to help. Until now, nobody has asked me what's wrong. Nobody has been concerned. Nobody has cared.

If you tell, nobody will believe you. If you tell, I'll hurt Sarah. If you tell, your father will be mad at you, Kat. You'll be the bad girl, Kat, like always. It's your fault, Kat. I can hurt you, Kat. You know they'll blame you, Kat. You can't even talk to them without arguing.

"Kat?" Scott's fingers tighten on my arm.

Greg's voice grows louder. *Kat, you're my special girl. Kat, nobody can know about how special you are — they'll be jealous and try to hurt you. Let me hold you. I can make you feel better.*

"Don't touch me!" I yell. I can't separate the touch on my arm from Greg's voice in my head.

Jerking free, I open the door and run down the driveway onto the road. A horn honks and headlights arc around me. I feel like I'm not really here, and this can't be happening.

"Kat!"

I draw in a deep breath at the sound of my name. Is that Scott's voice or Greg's? Greg gets angry if I try to run away. He'll punish me.

A dark cloak of panic wraps around me. Greg can't catch me. He can't touch me again. I can't stand anymore. I run up my driveway, my breath coming in short bursts. The fear of Greg popping out from behind every shadow and tree builds inside me.

Finally, the front door. I slam it shut behind me and look out the window. Nobody is coming up the steps and Greg's car is gone. I lean back against the door. *I'm safe. He's outside and can't get in.*

My breathing gradually slows to a more regular pace and the edges of panic start to fade.

"Get a grip, Kat," I tell myself.

Gradually, I start to notice my surroundings. The house is dark except for a lamp in the living room. Everybody must be in bed. That's odd. It must be later than I thought if the hockey game is over already and Dad is asleep.

Reality replaces the last edge of panic. Flinching, I remember what just happened outside with Scott. He must think I'm crazy. What happened to me out there? I think I'm going totally nuts.

"See what you've done to me!" I call out. Silence answers.

Chapter Eight

"Kat, Steph's here!"

Mom's voice, calling up the stairs, wakes me from a troubled sleep. I groan and roll over to see my alarm clock. Eleven o'clock already.

"Tell her to come on up here," I yell back.

I had tossed and turned all night, disturbed by weird dreams. First, Greg was chasing me through a park. He turned into a lion when he leaped on me. Steph was sitting on a park bench, laughing and watching the whole thing.

Then I had a dream about Scott. I asked him to help keep Greg away. Scott took me away and hid me. I begged him not to leave me alone, but he turned into Greg, promising he would always be with me.

My head is pounding, and I'm not looking forward to seeing Steph.

The bedroom door creaks as Steph peeks around it.

"Hey, can I come in?" She looks like she survived last night's party. The happy expression on her face makes me sick to my stomach.

I sit up on the side of the bed and shrug. "Suit yourself."

Steph steps in and closes the door behind her. "Guess you're mad about last night." She sits on my desk chair and rolls back and forth, pushing herself with her foot.

Is she for real?

Steph assumes the obvious by my silence and launches into a pitiful apology.

"Come on, Kat. I'm sorry I left you alone at the party, but you didn't seem to mind with that guy sprawled across your lap."

I glare at Steph. "That was a drunken jerk who fell on me. He spilled a drink all over me. I wouldn't exactly call that fun."

I point to the shirt lying on the floor. Steph picks it up and crinkles her nose.

"Sorry Kat. I didn't realize you were having such a miserable time. I'll make it up to you. I promise. Besides, how can you stay mad at me?"

Steph's face transforms into a goofy pout that makes me laugh. She's right. I can't stay mad at her. I really need a friend right now. Scott probably thinks I belong in the loony bin.

Steph smiles when I laugh. "I'm glad you're not going to give me a hard time. Scott already lit into me this morning for going to a party like that, for dating Mike, and for abandoning you. He was in a real mood. He's such a stick lately!"

Grabbing my dirty shirt away from Steph, I throw it in the corner and go to my closet to find some clothes. "He was worried about you. Give him a break. Some of the people there last night don't have the best rep."

"He's my twin, not my father," Steph moans. "He used to be fun, but lately he needs to loosen up."

I pull out a sweatshirt and an old pair of jeans. The shirt has been worn so much, it has holes in the elbows, but it's comfortable. The jeans have a hole in the right knee.

Steph wrinkles her nose. "Why don't you wear that shirt I bought you for your birthday?"

"Steph, you're only forgiven if you lay off about my clothes. These are comfortable, and I don't have plans today, anyway."

"Okay, okay. Deal. Hey, you wouldn't want to help me with that calculus assignment we're supposed to have done for Monday, would you?"

Sighing, I nod. Steph started asking for my help with homework a lot last year. I get the feeling she'd prefer I do it for her. That's probably why she asks me instead of Scott.

"Thanks," she says and jumps off the chair. "I'll get my books." The front door slams a few moments after Steph leaves my room.

I head for the kitchen, grab a bagel, and wander toward the family room, where Sarah is watching Saturday morning cartoons.

"Where are Mom and Dad?"

"They left when Steph came. They told me to get you if I needed anything."

Nice of them to let me know.

"Where'd they go?"

Sarah shrugs. "Don't know. They just said they'd be back soon. Jared called last night."

"Really?" I'm disappointed to have missed his call.

Her eyes light up. "Yeah, he said I can come visit him some time. That'll be neat."

"Yeah, that'd be cool. Maybe I'll try to call him."

Sarah turns back to the television. I try Jared's number. No answer.

A knock on the door echoes through the house as Steph bursts in. "I'm back," she shouts.

No kidding.

"Come upstairs. We might as well work in my room."

Steph and I spend the afternoon together. We do a bit of homework and Steph whines about having to learn derivatives. She can't think of a single time she'd ever have to use them in the "real world." I can't think of a use for them either, but I don't mind learning them.

We take a break from calculus and watch *Finding Nemo* with Sarah. After the movie, the phone rings.

Sarah answers in the kitchen, then returns to announce that Mom and Dad won't be home for a while.

"Where are they?" I ask.

"Dad is at Greg's, helping him fix their car. Mom did some work at the school and then went shopping with Amy."

"Great," I mumble.

"Mom said to order pizza for supper. We can use the money on top of her dresser."

"You want to stay for pizza?" I ask Steph. "You could stay over tonight. It'd be fun."

Steph shakes her head, glancing at her watch. "I can't. I'm going out with Mike."

"Oh." My stomach sinks. Scott is right – Mike is bad news. I nod my head toward my bedroom, signaling Steph that we need to talk away from Sarah.

She follows me up to my room.

"Um, Steph, maybe…"

"Oh, Kat, he's so great. We had a blast last night. He's so funny," Steph gushes. "He's an awesome kisser." Steph's eyes glow.

Caught off guard by her last statement, I clear my throat. "Oh…that's great, Steph. You didn't…?"

She catches my meaning immediately, and laughs. "No, of course not. We just made out. He made me tingle all over, Kat. I can't wait to see him tonight."

The guy is a jerk and doesn't deserve her. The thought of her "tingling all over" is sickening.

"Steph, maybe you should be kind of careful. He has a lousy reputation. What if he's using you or something?"

"Mike likes me for me, not for anything else. I can't believe you'd say something like that. What kind of friend are you?"

"Steph, I didn't mean it like—"

"Are you jealous? Is that your problem? Are you jealous that I attract guys and you don't?"

I grab Steph's arm. "Steph, that's not…"

Steph breaks away from my grip and paces around the room. "Scott said you freaked out on him last night. I just figured it was from the party. Maybe I'm wrong. Maybe it's more. You have been moody lately."

"I'm not jealous, Steph. Why would I be jealous over someone like Mike?"

"So now Mike's not good enough for you? Nobody's good enough for you lately."

Sudden anger clouds my common sense. "Yeah, you're right. *Nobody's* good enough for me." I look pointedly at Steph.

"Fine," Steph shouts and opens the bedroom door.

"Yeah fine," I shout back. "You better get ready for your *date*. It'll take awhile to make yourself beautiful."

Steph glares at me before leaving the room. I can hear her stomping all the way down the stairs and the front door slamming behind her.

How dare she yell at me and accuse me of being jealous! *Stupid, ungrateful…*

"What's her problem?" Sarah asks, stepping into my room.

"Nothing. What do you want?"

"Mom said you're supposed to order pizza. I'm hungry," Sarah whines.

"Fine." I push past her to get the pizza money from Mom's dresser.

"I'm telling Dad you pushed me," Sarah yells.

"Go ahead, you tell him everything. You always run to Daddy." I feel tight and ready to explode after my scene with Steph.

"I do not," Sarah screams at me.

"Yes, you do. You always go crying to him."

"Well, you're mean and bossy." Sarah sticks out her tongue.

"Shut up, Sarah."

"No, I don't have to. You can't make me. You're always telling me what to do, and I don't have to do what you say."

"Says who?"

"Says Daddy. He told me I don't have to do what you say when you're being silly, like when you told me to get away from Greg."

This whole argument has turned serious now that Sarah has mentioned Greg. I try to calm myself with a deep breath.

"Sarah, listen to me…"

"No, I don't have to. I'm not listening." Sarah covers her ears. "La-la-la-la-la-la-la-la-la—"

I pull her hands away from her ears. "Don't be so childish. Listen, I'm serious." I fight against Sarah's struggles to break free. "Sarah, you shouldn't be hugging Greg like that. You shouldn't be touching him at all or letting him touch you. Do you understand? Has Greg ever tried to touch you or hurt you, Sarah?"

Sarah begins to sob. "No, Kat. I'm not listening! Daddy says I can hug Uncle Greg whenever I want."

"Sarah!" I say harshly. "You can't do that anymore with Uncle Greg."

With a tug, Sarah breaks free and runs away. "You're not nice, Kat. I hate you."

Her steps echo down the stairs and the back patio door slides open. Let her pout. I'm ordering the pizza. If she's going to be a baby, then she can starve.

I calm down while I wait for the pizza. I didn't handle that well. If only she hadn't come in right after my argument with Steph, things probably would have gone better. I might have been able to make her understand how important it is for her to tell me if Greg has done anything to her.

"I'm only trying to protect you, Sarah," I whisper, just as the doorbell rings.

Pizza in hand, I search for Sarah. I'm annoyed when I don't find her on the swing. She does this all the time for attention. She's probably sitting on the rock ledge beside the fire pit, pouting like a baby.

Annoyance turns into anger, then worry, when I don't find her on the rock ledge, in the clubhouse, or down by our dock in the river. Sarah has disappeared.

Chapter Nine

"Scott? Steph? Please, somebody answer!" I shout, banging on their front door. I turn around, sagging against the door. *Now what?*

I try to stop sobbing, but it's a losing battle. It seems all I do lately is cry.

I almost fall when the door opens behind me.

"Jeez, Kat. What's up?" Scott catches me under the arms before I land on the porch.

"Scott…I need help." I gasp in air, trying to control my sobs.

"What happened?" Scott steadies me and turns me to face him.

"Sarah's gone. I can't do anything right. Steph is mad at

me. So is Sarah….She's mad at me…. *Everybody* is mad at me, and she's gone."

Staring into his concerned face, my knees buckle and I sag again. His grip on my arms tightens, stopping me again from falling.

"She's gone, Scott. She ran out of the house and disappeared. I didn't handle it very well. I didn't handle it well at all."

"We'll find her. I'll help you. Okay?"

I nod my head. Scott grabs my hand and leads me across the road to my house. "Think," he says, looking back at me. "Where would she go?"

"I don't know." I shake my head.

"Let's start back here." Scott leads me toward the backyard.

It's a relief to let Scott take charge of the situation. For once, I can just follow without making any decisions.

Scott pulls me along, the freshly cut grass clinging to my shoes. The setting sun stretches the tree shadows down to the river beside our property.

It'll be dark soon and we have no idea where Sarah is. Mom and Dad will shoot me and ask questions later. Guilt, worry, and anger wage war inside me.

"Do you think she would be in there?" Scott points toward the clubhouse.

"No. I already looked in there."

"Let's check again, anyway." Scott pulls me toward the clubhouse. Selfishly, I hope she's not there. The clubhouse is my private spot – my sanctuary – and I don't want to share it. My heart skips a beat when we come to the door. I hold my breath as Scott looks inside, releasing it when he shakes his head. She's not there.

"It's getting dark. Let's call her. Maybe she'll answer." Scott gives my hand a reassuring squeeze and calls Sarah's name.

"Sarah!" We take turns yelling her name, but the only reply is the occasional squawk of a bird and the plop of a fish jumping in the river.

Another voice rings out across the evening shadows. My father calls my name and then Sarah's. They would have to come home now. My pulse rate increases, and my ears ring at the thought of telling Dad that Sarah is gone.

"I guess I better tell them." I pull away from Scott trying to spare him from the inevitable confrontation.

"I'll go with you." A strange emotion clouds Scott's eyes, but I'm too focused on my inner panic to question it.

We run up the riverbank and across the lawn. As we approach, Mom steps through the patio door with Amy and Greg following behind her.

Oh, no. Not Greg. I can't deal with him right now. My feet feel like lead and I can't lift them.

"Scott, I can't. You tell them. Please."

Scott pulls me by the hand. "I'll be here with you. It'll be fine."

I shake my head. "I can't, Scott."

"What's going on, you two?" Dad demands. Greg steps up beside him and watches me with narrowed eyes.

Scott looks at me, waiting for me to speak. I stare back,

pleading with my eyes. I try to position his body in front of mine, shielding me from Greg and my father.

"Kat, what is it?" Mom asks.

"Mr. and Mrs. Thompson…" Scott begins. Dad's eyes swing from me to Scott. "Um…Sarah seems to have run away."

My father's eyes return to me, burning a hole through my skin. I expect to smell smoke and burning flesh any second.

"Is this true?" he demands, as if Scott would lie about something like this.

Nodding my head, I look down, avoiding the condemnation in his eyes.

My mother's gasp draws my attention toward her.

"What happened, Kat? What did you do to make her run away?" Dad's voice is laced with venom.

My eyes remain focused on Mom. If she looks at me the same way Dad did, I won't be able to take it. Scott takes another step forward. "Mr. Thompson…to be fair, she—"

"*Fair?* Kat seems determined to give her sister a hard time. Kat doesn't want to be fair to Sarah or anybody else living under this roof. So being fair to Kat is not my top priority right now."

Greg puts his hand on my dad's shoulder. "Now Dave, take it easy. We don't even know what's happened. We need to concentrate on finding Sarah right now."

I stare at Greg, trying to read what this will cost me. Why would he want to help me? Just when I think I hate the guy, he turns around and becomes the Uncle Greg I want him to be.

Amy approaches, putting her arm around my shoulder.

Most of the backyard is cast in shadow. In another ten minutes we won't be able to see each other without the patio light on.

"Where have you and Scott looked?" Amy asks.

I remain silent. I'm not surprised that Dad blames me, but I did not expect him to be so – well – so cold. How could he say something like that in front of everyone? He just announced that he doesn't give a damn about me, or my feelings.

"Kat?" When I look up, Greg is standing in front of me. His hand touches my shoulder. After Dad's words hitting me like an ice cold shower, Greg's touch feels welcome. He cares, and my father doesn't.

I watch my Dad pace across the patio. My mother tries to stop him with an outstretched hand. He brushes it away, ignores her, and continues marching around, mumbling to himself. His hands rake through his hair while he glares toward me every few seconds.

Mom whispers something to him.

"No, I will not calm down!" my father shouts. He kicks one of Mom's petunia pots. Dirt and a rainbow of pinks and purples fly through the air. The flowers land on the ground, close to my feet.

Scott grabs my hand. "Come on, let's go search by the river."

Greg holds up his hand. "Hold on. Let's organize this and do it properly. We'll all split up."

Greg turns to Dad. "Dave, we'll go down by the river together."

I'm grateful to Greg for getting my father out of here. If anybody can handle his temper right now, it's him.

My dad stares at Greg with narrowed eyes. Everybody is quiet, waiting to see what he'll do. My breath releases when he says, "Fine," and strides toward the river.

Greg watches Dad walk away then says to Amy. "Honey, you take Maria with you and go around to the neighbors. Maybe they've seen her."

Amy nods. She and Mom walk away, arms around each other.

Greg starts sprinting after my father.

"What about us?" yells Scott.

Greg turns. We can hardly see him anymore in the last of the evening light. "You guys grab a flashlight and look around the property. Don't go too far into the woods." Greg points toward the trees bordering the back of the yard before turning and disappearing over the riverbank.

I go into the house for a flashlight. Scott is waiting for me on the patio when I return.

"Let's go." I turn on the light and we follow its beam across the yard.

"Sorry to drag you into this." I stare at the beam of light, embarrassed to look at Scott after my dad's outburst.

"Not a problem. I wasn't sure if I'd see you again after…" Scott's voice trails off.

"Watch that tree root." I point with the flashlight at a large tree root sticking out of the ground.

"After the other night?" I ask, completing Scott's sentence.

I stop and point the flashlight up into the trees. Would Sarah climb up and get stuck?

Scott's footsteps stop beside me.

"Well, yeah. It was kind of weird. It was like I did something that freaked you out."

I start walking again, still looking up at the branches. Scott shuffles along beside me.

"Ouch," I yelp, stubbing my toe on a large stone.

Scott grabs my elbow so I don't fall.

"Thanks, I'm okay. Guess I better keep the light on the ground."

"What did happen?"

I try to distract him and change the subject. "You mean with Sarah tonight?"

"No, I'll let you save that one for your dad. I don't envy you having to deal with him later."

I snort in agreement.

"What happened to you the other night?"

I point the light at a grouping of evergreens. "Why don't we look over there? She could be hiding behind one of those."

"Fine."

He sounds annoyed. I don't want him to be mad at me. He's the only friend who will talk to me right now. My stomach tenses at the thought of losing both Scott and Steph.

"It was nothing," I finally answer him. "I guess I had a strange dream or something that freaked me out."

Scott grunts. "It must've been some dream." When I don't answer, he grunts again and tells me to forget it.

I flash back to my dream of Greg turning into a lion.

I know I need to give Scott some kind of an answer. "Yeah, it was about lions and tigers and bears." Last night's dream reaches out its claws, trying to pull me back in, while the darkness of the evening closes in on me.

No, not again. I can fight this. I'm not going to flip out again. The claws begin to retract. My mind searches for some way to release myself from the grip of those claws.

"Lions and tigers and bears, oh my," I chant, starting to skip, desperately trying to chase the dream away. The flashlight's beam dances around in the dark, like a firefly trying to find its way home.

"You're nuts," Scott says and finally laughs at me skipping around him with the beam of light dancing through the trees.

The claws are gone, for now.

"Okay, Dorothy, let's find your sister and get out of Oz," Scott says.

"Perhaps if I tap my heels three times…" I stand on my tiptoes and tap the heels of my white sneakers just as Dad shouts our names.

The battery of the flashlight dies as we draw closer to the backyard and we hear voices carry through the evening air.

"Why don't you go inside with Sarah? I'll talk to Kat when she gets back." Greg sounds like he's trying to calm my dad.

"No, Greg, I'll deal with her." Dad's tone leaves little to the imagination as to how he plans on dealing with me. Scott pats my arm.

My mom's voice chimes in, softer and a little harder to

hear from where we are. "Come…David…has a way with Kat and can handle…"

"I don't mind, Dave. Go in and see to Sarah. Maria, if you don't mind, maybe you could go to where you and Amy split up and tell her Sarah is home and safe."

Greg is standing alone on the back patio, under the porch light when we emerge from the trees and cross the grass. At this moment, I'd rather deal with him than Dad, especially with Scott beside me.

"Come on," he motions with his arm. "We found her. She climbed that old willow tree about a mile down the river."

"You mean the one with all the branches hanging over the water on the Miller property?" Scott asks as we step onto the patio with Greg.

"Yeah, that's the one."

"Wow, that's deep water. Jared and I used to dive from those branches. She's lucky she didn't fall in," Scott says.

I shiver, thinking of Sarah disappearing in the dark water of the river without anybody knowing what happened to her. She may be a pain sometimes and act like a selfish brat, but the thought of something like that happening is unbearable. I really messed up.

All of this happened because I was trying to talk to Sarah about Greg. I can't believe I softened toward him earlier tonight. I let him reel me in again, like a fish biting at the first worm he dangles in front of me.

"Do you want me to stick around while you deal with your dad?" Scott's question draws me out of my thoughts.

"I'll be here for Kat. You go on home," Greg says, not even giving me a chance to answer.

"Okay, I guess." Scott sounds as surprised as I am about Greg telling him to leave, but I still stand there saying nothing. "I'll see you later, Kat." Scott pauses as if waiting for a response.

I snap out of my trance when he turns to walk away. "I'll walk with you." How else can I avoid being left alone with Greg?

Scott stops and waits. I take one step, and Greg's hand grabs the back of my shirt, hidden from Scott's view.

"I think we should go inside and get this over with, Kat." Greg's other hand sneaks under my shirt and rubs my back. A shudder of disgust runs through me. What was I thinking earlier to believe he was the nice Uncle Greg? Snakes never change.

Scott waves. "Sure, whatever. Good luck." He turns and walks away. How could he not see what Greg is doing?

I open my mouth to yell at him, wanting so badly to make him come back and help me, but nothing comes out. Embarrassment over the thought that Scott might have seen Greg's hand rubbing my bare back and fingering my bra strap, wins over my need to reach out for help. Scott would blame me. He would think I'm a slut for letting Greg touch me like this. It's better to let him go.

"Please don't," I plead, my back still facing Greg. Every slide of his hand up and down my back makes me feel more and more dirty.

His fingers start to fiddle with my bra, trying to undo it.

"No, I don't want you to." I can't stand the babyish voice that comes from somewhere inside me.

"Come on, Kitty Kat. You've kept me waiting. Didn't I tell you the other day that it's not over between us?"

I hate it when he calls me Kitty Kat. He has made me into his pet – one that obeys his every command before being rewarded with love and affection. My cheeks burn and I begin to feel flushed. Sweat gathers on my forehead.

Greg lets go of my shirt. I move to step away from him but he wraps his arm around my waist, his fingers circling around my stomach, pulling me a little farther from the porch light to the edge of the patio. His grip is like an iron bar, imprisoning me. Tears of anger and frustration gather in my eyes, as the knot inside my stomach tightens.

I try to push his hand away from my stomach, barely recognizing my own voice pleading with him to stop.

"Why not, Kat? After everything I've done for you, why not?" Greg murmurs in my ear and brushes his fingers across my skin. "I've handled your dad and told him I'd talk to you. He's with Sarah, where he really wants to be. He doesn't love you as much as her, but I'll always be here for you, Kat."

The feel of his breath as he whispers in my ear sends chills down my spine. My stomach starts to heave and I'm dizzy and nauseated. *Please let it be over quickly.*

The porch light blurs as the familiar floating sensation takes over. My gaze remains fixed on the corner of the house as my mind begins to black out. The surrounding sights and sounds fade as reality slides away from the private place I create for myself, where Greg does not exist. A piece of me goes to this private place every time Greg touches me. My private place is without dreams, people, thoughts, or worries – only darkness exists there.

"Greg, I've been looking all over for you. Are you ready?"

I jump at the sound of Amy's voice, returning from my black place with a jolt. She appears around the corner of the house and stops, staring at me and Greg.

I'm still in front of Greg, my back to him. Amy would be able to see Greg's arm wrapped around me. In the darkness can she see his hand under my shirt with my hand on top of his?

The trees stop rustling in the breeze, the crickets stop chirping, and the moon looks down on us, as if waiting for the drama to unfold. Amy must be able to hear my pounding heart over the sudden hush of the evening. Her eyes dart back and forth between Greg and me.

Greg squeezes me, as if giving me a friendly hug. "I was just trying to calm Kat down. She's upset about earlier."

His squeeze tightens, conveying a silent warning for me to play along.

"Is that so?" Amy looks directly at me.

"Yeah," I whisper. Tears of mortification pool in my eyes, and I look away from Amy.

"Let's get going." Greg steps out from behind me. The back of my shirt falls, covering my back.

Greg puts his hand on my arm in a fatherly gesture. "Like I said, Kat, don't worry. Sarah is safe and sound, and your dad has calmed down. Everything's fine."

Nodding, I watch him walk away, then glance at Amy. She's still staring at me, as if she can read my mind and heart.

Without another word, Amy turns and follows her husband, leaving me to drown in guilt and shame.

Chapter Ten

Breakfast the next morning is silent. Mom had to leave early and Sarah gives me an obvious cold shoulder. Dad and I glare across the table every once in awhile, but refuse to say anything after our argument last night. I still smart from being told once again how selfish and ungrateful I have been.

My whole family is crazy. Nothing makes sense anymore.

Sarah can do no wrong in Dad's eyes, yet all she seems to want to do is sit in front of the television and disappear into some fantasy land. Jared, the champion in my Dad's eyes, is following in good old David Thompson's footsteps – lining the walls with trophies and attending university to become a lawyer and join the law firm.

Mom is there whenever Dad needs something, otherwise

he doesn't really say a whole lot to her – at least not when I'm around. He's too wrapped up in the sports section of the newspaper, or hanging out with Princess Sarah. When he's not home, he's wining and dining some new client.

Where do I fit in? I ask myself this question as I leave the house to walk to the hospital. It's not the first time I've wondered.

A horn beeps behind me. I wave at Scott while he signals to pull over beside the curb.

"Hey, everybody settled after last night?" Scott asks through the open window.

"I guess so. Sarah's sucking up the extra attention like a sponge." I roll my eyes.

Scott chuckles. "Yeah, she's always been good at that."

"No kidding." I look away for a moment, trying to contain my annoyance with Sarah. "Thanks for your help last night. I guess I kind of panicked."

"No problem. What are friends for?"

I turn and stare at Scott, noticing him in a different way. He has a beautiful smile, with small dimples that curl up with the corners of his mouth. When we were younger, he was embarrassed about his dimples. I had forgotten about them until now. I guess it's like a work of art. If you stare at it every day, you stop noticing the small details and eventually forget to appreciate the beauty behind it.

Raising my eyes from his dimples, I know what I'll see; brown eyes, alive and dancing with light. He's the only guy

I've ever met who could not only smile with his lips, but with his eyes as well.

Scott's cell phone rings and breaks the spell. I shake my head, trying to focus my thoughts again. Scott watches me with a strange look.

He picks up his phone. "Hello?" He holds his finger up, motioning for me to wait. "Okay, Steph. I'll be there in five minutes." Scott hits the "End" button and throws the phone on the passenger seat beside him, still not looking away from me.

"I have to pick up Steph. She feels bad she wasn't around last night."

"Yeah, right," I say under my breath. I didn't mean to say that out loud.

Scott's eyebrows lift. "Hey, don't worry about it," he says. "It's between you two. Keep me out of it! You guys will work it out – you always do."

"Sure," I say. We always worked it out when it was just me in the picture. Now Steph has somebody else to occupy her time. She doesn't need me anymore.

"I have to go. Steph's waiting, and she'll shoot me if I'm late."

"Okay, thanks again for last night. See you."

Scott pulls away and disappears around the next corner. He really does seem different lately. He's been blowing hot and cold. Sometimes he seems to be avoiding me, but other times he is the Scott he used to be, only more intense. Sighing, I enter the hospital and walk up to the pediatric ward.

"Kat, you're here! Thanks for coming in." Aunt Sheila grabs my arm and directs me to an empty room. "I need to talk to you."

She closes the door behind us. This is serious if she needs privacy to talk to me about my duties for a shift. I sit on the edge of the hospital bed, running my hand over the white sheet. Aunt Sheila paces in front of me.

"There are some terrible people in this world, Kat. As a doctor, I've seen some dreadful things done to children, but sometimes it's too close to home."

Sheila looks away, staring out the window. What could have happened? I've never seen her so agitated. Her gaze swings back to me.

"Why do you kids think we can't see what's happening in front of our noses? I spoke with your mom, Kat. I know what's going on, and I can't be wrong."

I freeze. *How could she know? How could she possibly know what Greg has done to me?* I feel faint, thinking about Sheila speaking to my mother about Greg. Why wouldn't Mom stay to talk to me this morning? Why didn't she hug me and tell me that it's okay because she still loves me? Why didn't she promise she would side with me over him any day?

An image of Greg's hands touching me last night flashes through my head. I worked so hard this morning to block that out and not think about it. The embarrassment of Amy finding Greg with his hands on my skin makes me feel like I'm going to throw up. Anybody seeing that would have a hard time believing that I didn't want him touching me. Nobody would take my side. Would they?

"Sheila, I need to explain—"

"She's here," Sheila interrupts me. I'm confused about who Sheila is talking about.

I sit straight on the bed again and look at Sheila. "Amy's here?" Amy is the only person I can think about who would confront me with what happened.

Aunt Sheila looks at me. "Amy? Why would Amy be here? Does she know Taylor?"

"Taylor? She's back?" My heart pounds, as I wait for her answer.

Sheila nods and starts pacing again. "She looks awful. He really did a number on her this time, and they can't explain this one with a fall."

Relief floods through me. She didn't speak to my mom about Greg. *She doesn't know what's happening.*

Sheila stops pacing again. "I had to talk to your mom, Kat. Of course, I can't tell her what has happened, but I had to find out what she thinks of the man. Am I way off base this time? I figured that people would have to see what he's really like. Your mom works with him every day. She sees him interact with kids at the school, yet she didn't have one bad thing to say about him. Worst of all, she says the kids love him and he loves them. How could such a brute put on a front like that?"

You have no idea, Aunt Sheila, how big a front some people can put on. I remain silent, stunned at the anger my usually laid-back Aunt is displaying. I'm shocked that Mom could be so blind. She would never believe me if I told her about Greg.

"We need to get Taylor to talk, Kat. It's the only way we can help her. I've had the family investigated once, but Taylor wouldn't talk and her injuries seemed to match their story. I'll do it again because I'm sure I'm right about this one. I don't think anything will happen unless she talks."

"How bad is she?"

"She's pretty black and blue. She has a concussion and two broken ribs. No child is klutzy enough to fall down the steps twice in such a short period of time. Her arm isn't even healed yet, for Pete's sake."

Aunt Sheila continues, "Nobody deserves that. Every child is beautiful and special and deserves love and protection. It disgusts me that people can get away with something so terrible."

For the first time since I can remember, a sensation of warmth wraps my heart, hugging me and helping me feel safe.

"Do you really believe that, Aunt Sheila?" My voice cracks with the hope I'm trying to control.

"Of course, I do. Children are a gift, and it's our job to teach them, love them, and nurture them."

Aunt Sheila would believe me, no matter what. Her words prove it.

"Aunt Sheila, I need to tell you—" I'm interrupted by the buzz of the paging intercom.

"Dr. Williams, please report to room two twenty-three. Dr. Williams," a voice commands.

Sighing, Aunt Sheila rubs her hand over her face. Is her

hand shaking? She looks so pale. The bags under her eyes are larger than usual. She looks ten years older than the last time I saw her.

"I'm sorry, Kat, but we'll have to talk about this later. I don't usually lose it like this but this case gets to me. So many people have children exposed to this monster at the school. Could you work with Taylor today and see if she'll tell you anything? She really missed you after you left the first time. You two obviously connected."

I nod. "Sure, I'll do what I can."

I sit on the bed for a few minutes, trying to digest everything that has happened in the last few minutes, before going to Taylor's room. I feel like I've jumped on an emotional roller coaster. Going from the fear that Sheila knew about Greg to actually wanting to tell her about him was confusing and frightening. This secret that I have guarded for so many years is becoming a heavy burden. Do I have the right to unload it on Aunt Sheila, who is suffering enough with Taylor and all the other kids who depend on her care?

Aunt Sheila is worried that Mr. Bradford is around other kids all the time. What if my own silence means that Greg has hurt other kids? I've been worried about Sarah, but never thought of others I haven't been able to protect.

A light knock sounds on the door and Wanda peeks in. "Hi, Kat. Your Aunt asked me to let you know what room Taylor's in."

I follow Wanda down the hall. It's a quiet day on the ward,

with only the sound of the occasional television coming from one or two of the rooms. Usually you can hear a child or baby crying, but not today.

Wanda stops in front of the last door.

"Taylor's alone right now. Her mother hasn't been here watching over her little lamb this time. Nobody has been up to see the poor kid since she was admitted last night. It's weird after the last time. Her mother wouldn't leave her side then."

"Thanks, Wanda." I open the door to peek inside. Wanda's footsteps fade down the hall while I stand there staring at the still shape on the bed.

The bed is slightly inclined. Taylor's head is turned away from me, toward the window. Maybe she's sleeping. Her hair is spread across the pillow in a tangled mess.

"Taylor, it's Kat. Are you awake?" I walk around the bed so I can see her face. Tears are sliding down her cheeks.

I squat down in front of the bed, wiping her tears away with my finger.

"Hi, Taylor. I'm going to sit with you, and you can just cry as hard as you want, if it makes you feel better."

"I can't cry. It hurts," Taylor whispers.

"Okay." I run my hand over her hair, flinching at the knots and tangles. Nobody has looked after her in days.

"How about I brush your hair and we can tell stories? I missed telling stories to you."

"I didn't want the nurses to touch me. They hurt me when they move me around. I don't want to talk to them."

"I know, but they're just trying to help you."

Taylor looks into my eyes. "Will you brush my hair, Kat? You're nice. You won't hurt me. You can tell me a story. I liked pretending you were my sister."

I close my eyes, my hand resting on the top of Taylor's head. "You're right, Taylor. I won't hurt you. Nobody will hurt you anymore," I promise.

Chapter Eleven

Friday, September 15.
Taylor's fear of the nurses really got to me last weekend. She hardly spoke when I brushed her hair. She just lay there.

I told her a story of a little girl who was special but who was being hurt by a mean man. The little girl was brave because she no longer let the man hurt her.

I could tell Taylor was listening because she started crying while I talked. She seemed much calmer at the end of the story and fell asleep when I finished.

I shiver from the cold breeze drifting through the clubhouse window. The hot weather we were having at the beginning of

September has given way to cool, wet days.

I get up to close the window. Sarah is on the swing. What's she doing outside on a cold day like this? Usually she stays in front of the TV.

I stand and watch Sarah through the window and picture myself, swinging from the tree. At Sarah's age, I was in denial that anything Greg was doing could be wrong. I felt strong and loved.

When Greg married Amy, I began to feel that things weren't right. I was eight at their wedding and confused. Why was he marrying Amy if he loved me and called me his special girl? I was jealous of Amy and misbehaved when she came to the house.

Amy was patient and eventually won me over. She'd take me to the movies and do things with me that my parents never had time for. She would talk about Greg and how happy they were.

That's when the guilt started. Greg was still calling me his special girl. I felt disloyal to Amy and hated myself for it.

But it wasn't your fault, a voice inside me whispers. I've heard this voice before, but ignored it, lost in my own guilt and confusion.

Could it be true? How could it be my fault any more than it is Taylor's for what her father is doing to her?

"Hi, Amy!" Sarah's squeal brings me back to the present.

Fidgeting with my hands, I watch Amy cross the yard. This can't be good. Mom and Dad aren't home, so Amy hasn't come to see them.

Amy walks over to Sarah and pushes her on the swing. Sarah giggles at something Amy says, and jumps off the swing. "See you later," Sarah yells, running toward the house.

Amy stares at the clubhouse. Can she see me peeking through the curtain? I hold my breath, wondering what she'll do. If I'm quiet, maybe she'll go home. No such luck; Amy walks toward the clubhouse.

I start to panic. I'm sure Amy saw something between Greg and me the other night, even though it was dark. I swallow hard, refusing to let her see me nervous and sick.

Bracing my hands on the wall in front of me, I try to prepare myself. *Play dumb, Kat. Act like everything's okay.*

When I turn to look toward the door, I realize my journal is still on the table. The blood rushes to my head when I hear Amy's footsteps outside the door. *I have to get rid of it!* I grab the journal and throw it behind the milk crates a split second before Amy appears in the door.

"We need to talk, Kat."

Turning to Amy, I try to think of an excuse to avoid this confrontation. I'm shaking and still breathing heavily from the fear that she might have seen my journal. I don't think she saw me throw it before she came in.

"Now's not good, Amy. I have to meet Steph." I try to walk past her, but she reaches out and grabs my arm.

"Steph can wait. We need to talk about this."

I back away and her hand falls from my arm. I feel as if I've been burned.

"I want to know what's going on. I've heard Greg out, now

I want to hear what you have to say. You've both been acting strange, and I want to know why."

A million thoughts race through my head and I can't hold on to any of them. *What do I do? Please let me just disappear. Please let this be a dream. Stall her. Change the subject. Distract her. What did Greg say to her?*

"Now, Kat."

"What…what did he say?" My head spins and the floor tilts to one side, trying to tip me over.

"I want to hear what *you* have to say. What did I see between you and Greg?"

"N-n-nothing," I say, trying to speak past the lump in my throat. How can I describe what's been happening? How can I explain what would have happened if she hadn't shown up? The pain in my stomach clinches my insides with every breath, until I can barely stay on my feet.

"Do you think I'm blind…or stupid?" Amy's voice rises in frustration. Her arms are on her hips. She looks tense and ready to grab me at any moment. I've never seen such a cold look in her eyes.

I remember the excuse Greg gave when Amy appeared. "He was trying to make me feel better. That's it, Amy. I don't know…I don't know what else you think there could be." The words gush out so fast I can barely understand them.

"Do you have feelings for Greg, Kat?"

"Feelings? What do you mean?"

"How do you feel toward Greg?" Amy asks again.

I shrug. How can I tell her how I feel about Greg when I

don't even know? The cramping in my stomach is stronger. I have to fight the urge to drop to my knees and curl into a little ball. My face burns with shame.

"He's like an uncle to me, if that's what you mean."

Amy is quiet for a moment. Did she hear me? Does she believe me?

"Do you feel the same way as you do toward Jared?"

"I…I guess so," I reply. I know what she's getting at.

"Either you do or you don't." Amy clenches her hands into fists and takes a step toward me.

I back away from her. Will she threaten me like Greg? The wall of the clubhouse blocks me from moving any farther and supports me as I lean against it, my knees no longer able to support all my weight.

"I saw your hand holding his against you. Can you explain that to me? That's *not* something you would do with Jared."

Closing my eyes, I try to picture the scene Amy interrupted. Yes, my hand was on Greg's. I was trying to keep it from touching me; trying to force it away from me. I swallow and fight the blackness whirling around me.

"That's not how it was. I was trying—"

Amy holds up her hand. "Stop, I don't want to hear lies. Greg told me what's going on. He explained everything, and I'm disappointed."

Thankful for the support of the wall behind me, I close my eyes and sigh. He told her. It's over. The blackness begins to fade and the pain in my stomach becomes a dull throb.

"How could you do that to Greg?"

Shocked at her words, my eyes fly open. "Do…do what?"

"He told me about your crush and your threats. You need help, Kat. I can understand an innocent crush, but to threaten to tell your parents he's coming on to you…that's a terrible thing to do. How could you, after everything we've done for you? Greg treats you like he would his own flesh and blood. He'd do anything for you and your family. He really thinks we can help you through this."

"It's not true, Amy…I wouldn't do that." I fight to stay above the whirling blackness underneath me. My head pounds and angry tears fall from my eyes.

"What's not true? Tell me the truth, Kat. I want to know what's going on, and I want to know now."

I clutch my stomach and groan, "No, no, no, no."

The clubhouse is spinning in circles. I close my eyes, trying to drown everything out.

The rustle of Amy's coat is closer, but I squeeze my eyes shut, not able to look at her. "It's over, Kat. No more of this. I'm going to talk to your parents."

"No," I repeat again. "It's not me. It's not my fault. It's him."

"No more lies. That's enough!"

"He threatens me. He makes me…He touches me."

"He told me you'd do this. Even after the way you've threatened him, he's still worried about you and only wants the best for you. He's trying to help you get through this, and now you say it's him. How dare you…"

I open my eyes, blinded for a brief moment by the sudden

burst of light. The look of contempt in Amy's eyes turns me cold inside.

Greg did this to me. Greg did this to her. I won't let him come between me and Amy.

"No! You're wrong," I shout, pushing her aside and darting toward the door. Something crashes to the floor, but I don't stop to look back.

Sobbing, I stumble along the riverbank, toward the trees. I hardly notice the bare tree branches snagging my hair and scratching my face.

I stumble over a root and fall to the ground, pain from the impact shooting up my arm. Curling myself into a ball, I burst into a torrent of tears. Everything I've trapped inside flows out, leaving me empty, cold, and trembling on the cold ground.

Hearing the words spoken aloud, in my own voice, has left me incapable of denying the truth. He really does do those terrible things. It's true, it's not a dream, and it's not right.

It's his fault, not mine. I was just a little girl. I'm still just a little girl.

My tears leave angry paths on my cheeks. My body reacts as the anger builds; I stop shaking, my heartbeat becomes less erratic, and the fear in my stomach subsides. I don't deserve the things that Amy said. I'm better than that. I'm better than *him*.

Chapter Twelve

It's been two days since Amy confronted me, and now the fear is back, even stronger than before. When is she going to tell my parents all of Greg's lies? When will I no longer be a part of this family?

I should just get to Mom and Dad first, and tell them myself. Why don't I?

I tried to talk to Mom yesterday, but she was busy with lesson plans. Last night when she asked if anything's wrong, I chickened out. The guilt was back. I couldn't destroy her with my problem, or, worse yet, I couldn't bear hearing her say what Amy said; she doesn't believe me.

I called Jared again, and he was actually there for once. I was hoping he would tell me that I'm fine and everything will be okay. But the words lodged in my throat. Jared talked about his perfect, busy life. When I hung up, my secret was still intact.

How can I find the right words when I'm not even sure I want to say them at all?

I twist myself around in circles on the swing in the backyard, staring at the dull, brown ground beneath my feet. A picture of Sarah sitting on this swing flashes through my head. She looked so innocent and carefree. Sarah – Daddy's little pet. If I so much as look at her the wrong way, I get in trouble.

Lifting my feet off the ground, I hold my legs in front of me and watch the world swirl in dizzying circles as the rope unwinds.

My hands are numb. The air is crisp and cool. The swing stops its dance and I bring my hands to my mouth to blow on them.

Sarah gets to be the little girl I never could be. She has the peace that comes with innocence, the trusting nature of somebody who doesn't have a worry in the world. *For now.*

"Kat, I'm driving to the library. Do you want a ride to the hospital?" Mom yells, stepping out onto the patio.

I glance at my watch. Wow. I'm supposed to be at work in fifteen minutes. I jump off the swing and rush past my mom, "Just give me a second to change."

The drive to the hospital is quiet. It's like we're two strangers, not knowing what to say to each other.

"See you," I say before slamming the door and running through the hospital entrance. I can't shake the feeling that I just gave up a perfect opportunity to make things better.

Sighing, I head for the elevators.

Wanda is sitting at the nurses' station.

"Hey, Wanda. How's your little one?" I ask, eager for a distraction.

Wanda's eyes always light up when she talks about her daughter. "She said a new word last night. After dumping her bowl of spaghetti over her head, and onto the floor, she looked at me and said 'bad.' She had spaghetti in her ear, on her clothes, in her nose, hanging from her hair, and on the dog. I didn't know what to clean up first."

I smile at the image of Wanda's one-year-old covered in spaghetti.

"I'm wrapped around her little finger. But she has her daddy right where she wants him, too. He just goes to mush when she turns those baby blues on him, no matter what she's done."

"Too bad all dads can't be like that with their little girls."

"You're not kidding. Your little friend is still here." Wanda looks down the hall at Taylor's room.

"She won't talk to any of us. Her family still hasn't been in to see her, which is really odd. We've all tried to talk to her, but she doesn't want anything to do with us. She's closed herself off."

"What does Aunt Sheila say?" I ask.

"She's at a loss. I don't think Taylor said one word to the social worker who was here."

"What will happen?"

"I think that they'll try to assess what kind of risk Taylor is facing, especially since this is the second time we've called. I don't know what will happen if she doesn't talk, though."

I nod and look toward Taylor's closed door. "Should I go see her, or let her be?"

"It can't hurt to try. If she doesn't want you there, you'll know soon enough."

"That's true, I guess. See you later."

"Good luck. You're going to need it."

I push the door open with sweaty palms and hesitate when I hear Taylor's sobs. I start to close the door. I can't even deal with my own problems. How can I possibly help Taylor?

Taylor sees me before I get the door completely closed. "Are you leaving me too?"

"Of course not. I wouldn't do that." I feel guilty for the lie I just told.

"Everyone else has," Taylor says, between sobs. "I don't want to cry. It hurts here, but I can't help it." She points at her ribs.

I enter the room and sit on the chair beside Taylor's bed, grasping her small hand.

"What do you mean, everyone has left you?"

"They don't want me anymore, Kat. He told me they wouldn't like me if I told the secret." Taylor sniffles. "But I didn't tell the secret. Why don't they like me?"

Taylor's eyes are sad and confused. "I didn't tell. I'm not a bad girl. I stopped talking to the doctor and nurses so I wouldn't tell. I didn't talk to the other lady who came in, either.

But now they're gone."

Tears course down Taylor's cheeks.

"Who's gone, Sweetie?" My throat burns as I fight to keep my own tears from gathering.

"Mom, Dad, and Darren. I didn't tell the secret. Why did they go?"

"They're not gone. They're just really busy and haven't been able to visit." *How could they do this to her?* My blood boils at the thought of how terrified Taylor must feel.

"Really?"

"Of course. They love you. They wouldn't leave you. We all love you, Taylor. We all want to see you get better."

Taylor squeezes my hand and closes her eyes. "Was Suzie brave for keeping her secret, Kat?"

Who's Suzie? Then I remember the last story I told her about Suzie, the brave little girl who wouldn't let the bad man hurt her anymore.

How do I answer her? She needs to believe that telling me is the right thing.

"Suzie was brave. She was even braver for sharing her bad secret with her mom."

"Did everybody leave her?" Taylor opens her eyes and stares into mine.

"No, nobody left her except the bad man. They loved her even more and stayed with her to make sure nobody ever hurt her again."

"How did she know her secret was bad?"

I think about how to answer Taylor.

"Secrets can be bad for lots of reasons. If the secret is about somebody being hurt, or if it hurts you, then it's bad. If somebody threatens you, then it's probably a bad secret that you should tell your mom about."

"You mean even if they say bad things will happen if you tell the secret?" Taylor asks.

"Yeah, exactly."

"What if Suzie didn't tell her secret?" asks Taylor.

"Then the bad man would've kept hurting her. He might even have been hurting other kids."

"So Suzie saved those other kids?"

I nod. "Suzie helped them by telling her secret."

"Can he hurt Suzie for telling the secret?"

I shake my head and squeeze Taylor's hand. "No, he can't. He's gone."

"What if Suzie misses him? What if the bad man is her dad?"

Oh gads. What should I say?

"Taylor, Honey…" Taylor's eyes are large and serious.

Squeezing her hand, I clear my throat. "Everyone is different, and that includes daddies. Some of them play sports with their kids. Some of them like to play and read to their kids. Some daddies work a lot and don't have as much time as they should for their kids, but they still come in and hug them and kiss them at night before they go to bed. Some daddies aren't very nice to their kids. And there are daddies who sometimes hurt their kids."

Taylor's grip tightens on my hand.

"What if a daddy does all of those things?" she whispers.

Shifting in the chair to face Taylor better, I lift her chin with my hand. She trembles from the effort of holding back tears.

"If a daddy does all those things, he's trying hard to be nice to his little girl, but he needs help. The little girl would be very brave if she wanted her daddy to get help. Special people can help that daddy learn how to be nice all the time."

"Why would people want to help?" Taylor asks.

"Because little girls and boys are special. People want to make sure they're protected and loved all the time so nothing bad happens to them."

Taylor looks out the window behind me. "Will they hurt my daddy?"

I swallow the lump in my throat. Does she realize what she's admitted?

"No, they won't hurt your daddy. They'll talk to him and help him get better. And they'll make sure he won't hurt you, or any other kids, again."

Taylor looks at me and nods. "That's what I want, Kat. I want Daddy to be nice all the time."

"Will you talk to Dr. Williams, Taylor? She needs to find the right people to help you."

Taylor stares silently at our hands, mine engulfing her smaller one. *Please say yes, Taylor. Let us help you.*

Chapter Thirteen

My bones feel like mush and I wish I could sleep for a week.

"You look tired. Are you okay?" Mom asks, glancing at me when she stops at a red light.

"Yeah." I close my eyes, hoping she'll take the hint. If I tell her about my day, she'll probably accuse Taylor of lying. Besides, I can't. I'm bound by patient confidentiality.

The muscles in my arms are still cramped from leaning over the bed and holding Taylor's hand while she poured her heart out to Aunt Sheila. My head pounds like a ticking time bomb.

I open my eyes and look out the window, thinking about the past few hours.

I can still see Taylor's haunted eyes when she denied everything after I asked her to talk to Aunt Sheila.

"We don't need help. We're happy."

My heart sank. She was going backwards. I struggled to control my panic and frustration. I squeezed Taylor's hand, trying to gather my thoughts. "I know you're happy. Wouldn't you like to be even happier?"

Taylor was silent for a moment. "I don't know."

"Would your very own Peter Rabbit book make you happier?"

Taylor nodded, the corners of her mouth lifting slightly.

"Okay. What about playing at the park? Would that make you happier?"

She nodded again.

I looked out the window, trying to figure out what else to say. Flaming red and orange leaves twirled down from the trees. *Of course, what kid doesn't like playing in the leaves this time of year.*

I looked back at Taylor. "You know what made me happy? Once I helped my dad rake the leaves on our lawn into a big pile, and then I jumped in them."

Taylor's eyes widened. "Did he get mad?"

"No, he jumped in with me." An image of Dad and me jumping in the leaves flashed through my head. It made me sad to realize we haven't had fun like that for so long.

Taylor's eyes grew even wider. "Really?" she whispered.

"Yeah, and then we raked them up and did it all over again. Would something like that make you happier?"

Taylor's awed expression disappeared. Her eyes glazed, and her face took on a ghost-like pallor. "My dad would get really mad. You must have a nice dad."

"Yeah, I suppose I do." Dad and I have our problems, especially with communication, but he's a good guy.

"Taylor, if we could get help for your daddy, he could learn how to control his anger. Then you could do everything we talked about, and more."

Taylor nodded and wiped her tears.

"Are you ready for me to call Dr. Williams?"

"Yes," she whispered.

"Well, we're home." Mom's voice brings me back to the present.

"Thanks for picking me up." I open the door and dodge into the house, avoiding any further conversation with Mom.

Dad is in his office, talking on the phone. I sneak to my room, closing the door behind me so I don't have to face anyone. Relieved, I flop on the bed and stare at the ceiling.

I can't believe so much could happen in a single day. Within a few hours, Taylor's life has changed forever.

My heart breaks for Taylor and what she is going through. But, for the first time in her life, things can only get better for her. I promised her that she would be able to jump into a pile of leaves as soon as she was stronger.

So why am I not feeling better?

I sit up and stare at the mirror as my image blurs and changes. A girl, who looks to be about six, stares back at me. She has blonde pigtails, a spattering of freckles across her nose, and two missing front teeth. She looks like any other child, except for the fear reflected in her eyes. A tear runs down the child's face. I reach up and feel wetness on my cheek.

Tenderness and love for this child fills me, just like it did the first time I saw Taylor.

"You don't deserve it, either. But I don't know how to help you," I whisper to the child.

Her sad face starts to fade. *No, don't go!*

I rise from the bed and approach the mirror. The child is gone, replaced by my reflection.

I have to fight for that little girl. She deserves a life without fear, too. She needs to play without listening for *his* voice. She needs to feel safe in her home without *him* walking through the door. She needs to know her parents will always love her and take her side over *his*.

That child is inside you. That child needs you right now.

I shake my head. That child is gone.

I can't think this through without my journal. I open the bedroom door to run to the clubhouse.

"Oh! You scared the wits out of me." Mom clenches her hand over her chest, her other hand offers the cordless phone.

"Sorry," I mumble, trying to step around her.

"Wait." Mom grabs my arm. "Steph is on the phone."

"Steph?" I ask stupidly.

"Yes." Mom studies me, her eyebrow raised in concern. "Are you okay?"

"Yeah." I take the phone and turn around to close the door again.

"You're welcome," Mom shouts when the door shuts in her face.

I haven't spoken to Steph since our last fight. *What can she want?*

Chapter Fourteen

I stare at the phone, afraid to answer it. If Steph starts talking about Mike, we'll argue again. But if she misses me as much as I miss her…

I sit on the bed and raise the phone to my ear. "Hello?" My voice croaks like a sick frog.

"Hi," Steph whispers.

Our breathing is the only thing breaking the silence between us. The phone is slippery in my sweaty palm. Why doesn't she say anything? Did she change her mind? Maybe I can't hear her over my pounding heart.

"How are you?" Steph finally asks.

How am I? I'm an emotional wreck. I feel lost and betrayed and I miss you like crazy. You haven't been here for me through any of this.

Shying away from voicing any of these thoughts, I shrug my shoulders as if she's in the room. "Fine. You?"

"Okay. Look – this is kind of awkward – maybe I could come over?"

"Why?" I don't want her here if we're going to fight again.

"Because I miss you, you dork," Steph says and then gasps. "I'm sorry. I didn't mean to say that."

I catch my breath. *Did she say she misses me?*

"Are you there? Kat?"

A bubble of laughter escapes. Trying to hold it in, I start to snort and then we're both laughing.

"I'll meet you at the front door," I gasp between giggles, and we both hang up.

I throw open the front door just as Steph runs up the driveway.

"Hey, Dork," she says, bounding up the steps. We laugh and hug, goofy grins plastered on our faces.

"I'm sorry," we both say in unison and collapse again into a fit of giggles.

"Come on upstairs." We run to my room. Closing the door, I grin at my best friend. It's so good to have her back.

"I'm sorry," she says. "I don't know how many times I picked up the phone to call you and chickened out. I was hurt that you didn't need me when Sarah disappeared—"

"That's not true! You weren't home. You were out with Mike." I flinch at saying his name.

"That's not fair…."

I hold up my hand. "It doesn't matter. You weren't home when it happened. It doesn't matter where you were."

Liar. You were upset that she was out with Mike when you needed her. Ignoring the voice inside my head, I flop down on the bed beside Steph. She has that look on her face, as if she is trying to hold something back.

"What?" I ask.

"Nothing."

"Come on. What's up? It'll kill you to keep your mouth shut."

Steph smiles before becoming serious. "You okay, Kat?"

I'm suddenly wary. *What does she know?*

"Of course I'm okay. What do you mean?"

"Well, Scott said you haven't been yourself lately."

"Scott doesn't know what he's talking about. Besides, why were you talking about me like that?"

"Don't get mad. I had to practically drag it out of him. I wanted to know how you were after Sarah's disappearing act. He told me that I should've come to see how you're doing. He's right. I'm sorry we fought."

I shrug, uncomfortable with this conversation.

"He told me you aren't yourself. At first he thought it might be because of our fight, but he thinks it's something more. He said that things were weird the other night with you and your parents and even Greg."

Panic begins to close in around me. *What did Scott see?* Everything begins to darken. *Concentrate, Kat. Stay with it.* I take a deep breath and force my mind to focus on Steph. I'm not ready to talk about it yet. If I tell, I can never go back. If I tell, I'll be the bad one.

"Kat?"

I force a smile. "Scott was imagining things. Everything's fine. The usual – you know, Sarah pulls a pout for attention, Dad immediately sides against me, and everything is my fault. And what would Scott know? I've hardly seen him lately." It takes all my concentration to keep my voice light.

"Yeah, he's been really moody at home, and for some reason he's hanging out with those Science geeks at school…. So that's it? Just the usual family chaos?"

I nod. "You know how it can be around here." I turn away to avoid Steph's eyes. Can I fool her after all our years of friendship?

"Yeah. How're things now?"

I shrug. "Don't know. I haven't been here much. Yesterday at breakfast I got the cold shoulder. Then I went to work and stayed late, so I haven't really seen either of my parents since."

"Why did Sarah take off?"

"We had a stupid argument about…pizza, and she had a hissy fit."

"Hmmm. Let's talk about more exciting things," Steph suggests, and I'm in total agreement, as long as those more exciting things have nothing to do with Mike.

We talk for over an hour about school, music, gossip, and anything else we can think of.

I even tell Steph about Taylor, without mentioning Taylor's name or who her family is.

"Wow, you mean this poor kid's father has been beating her and she's been afraid to tell anybody?" Steph plops a grape into her mouth.

"Yeah, he's been threatening her all along."

"But still, even after all the threats, she could have told somebody. What's her problem?"

My gut clenches. I mentally count to ten, trying to cool my anger at Steph's naïve question.

As if sensing my mood, Steph says, "Oh well, at least everything's for the best now. You actually made a difference in somebody's life. It sounds like she'd still be crying in that hospital bed if you hadn't helped her. That's cool."

I feel a bit better. I never thought of it that way. Who would have figured I could make a difference in somebody's life?

"Hmmm, I suppose."

"Hey, let's get out of here for awhile. Mike and some of his friends are hanging out down by the dam this afternoon. You want to go?"

I should have been prepared for Mike's name to come sooner or later, but I wasn't. I don't want to go hang out with him and his friends, but I'm not ready to lose Steph again, now that we're back on track.

"Come on, I really want you to get to know Mike. He's not that bad."

"Well…I guess so."

"Great! I have to run home and change. Hey, why don't I bring an outfit back for you?" Steph eyes my tattered sweats and pullover.

"I don't know. I'm kind of comfortable and…" I hesitate, thinking about the afternoon we've just had together. I feel good about making a difference in Taylor's life. I do want to help myself, so why not start with a new look?

An hour later, we leave the house and walk to the dam. It's only about a fifteen-minute walk from the house. That gives me time to adjust to the heels Steph insisted I wear.

With every step I take Steph's short skirt feels like it's hiking up my thighs. I pull down on it for what seems like the hundredth time, when Steph smacks my hand and tells me to stop fiddling.

"I can't help it. It feels like my butt is exposed to the world, and I'm cold." I shiver in her borrowed sweater. She wouldn't let me bring my coat because it doesn't match the skirt.

"Don't think about the cold, and you won't feel it," Steph says.

We continue the walk in silence; the only sound being the crunch of leaves under our feet. The musty smell of rotting fish and stale water grows stronger.

As we cross the bridge, Steph points to a group of people down by the dam. "There they are." She breaks into a jog, leaving the sidewalk and heading down the path.

"Steph, wait up," I yell, trying to jog in the heels.

My foot turns on a stone, knocking me off balance. I

sprawl face first into the mud. A pain shoots through my knee. The earthy, damp smell of dirt and wet leaves fills my nostrils, making me sneeze. I blush when Mike's friends laugh from their perch on the dam.

Steph's feet appear in front of my face. "Are you okay?"

She helps me up. Brushing dirt off my hands, I glance down to assess the damage. My skin is red and scraped around my knee.

"I think I'll just go home." *Why should I change who I am, anyway?*

"No, come with me. Face them and laugh with them and it'll be fine. *Please* come." Steph leads me back down the path. I follow, my body tight and my face burning with embarrassment.

"Hey, walk much?" a red-haired guy leaning against the cement wall of the dam yells.

"Ignore him. That's Tim. He thinks he's a real comedian, but nobody laughs at his jokes." Steph glances back at me with a reassuring smile.

"It seems like they're all laughing this time." I feel stupid and out of place.

"Hey everyone, this is Kat." Steph introduces me to the group when we join them at the ledge.

"Hey Kat, nice legs," a blond guy with a cigarette hanging from his mouth says.

"Her *legs*?" a guy with dark curls asks. "What about her ass? It looked pretty good sprawled in the dirt."

Mortified, I stare at the ground and realize that this stupid excuse for a skirt probably did ride up when I fell, exposing my butt for the world to see.

"Lay off, guys," Mike's deep voice commands. "Come here, Baby." I look up to see Steph being pulled toward Mike, like a rag doll. He gives her a kiss, running his hand over her rear.

"Come on you guys, get a room," a girl standing off to the side says, making faces at Steph and Mike. I didn't notice her when we first joined the group. Is that a joint hanging from her mouth? She glances my way, smiling slyly. "You want a drag?" She holds the joint toward me.

The last remnants of laughter fade while they all watch, waiting to hear what I'll say.

"I don't…"

"Come on guys, leave her alone. You'll scare her away." Mike snickers with a few of the other guys.

Steph punches Mike's arm. "Lay off."

Mike narrows his eyes at Steph. I back away from the girl who is still holding the joint toward me.

"Oh, that's okay. Not right now," I stammer. Why did I let Steph convince me to come?

Steph's eyes widen and she opens her mouth, pointing at something behind me. "Watch…"

I back up and trip over Tim's foot. For the second time within two minutes, I hit the dirt. This time I land on my rear, the impact jarring me enough that I bite my tongue. The salty taste of blood fills my mouth.

"Look guys, she's falling for me," Tim says to a chorus of laughter.

I turn to Steph with pleading eyes, hoping she'll help me out of this situation before I make an even bigger fool of myself.

Steph pulls away from Mike to come to my aid, but his hand snakes out behind her to grab the back of her jacket. I can't believe she likes to hang out with these jerks. Obviously preserving her image with them means more to her than our friendship.

"Hey, Princess, let me give you a hand." Tim reaches out to me.

"Forget it." I slap his hand away. "I'd rather be touched by a snake than let you take my hand."

"Ooohhhh! The princess has claws." Tim backs away, pretending to be scared. Everybody chuckles, except Steph. She stares blankly, with Mike holding her in place like a master controlling his puppet.

I get up and brush the dirt off my behind. I look at each one of them, hating myself for letting them intimidate me, until my gaze stops on Steph. I've lost her to these idiots, who don't deserve her. Anger lends me the confidence I need to walk away with some pride.

"Call me if you ever get sick of these jerks." Their taunts follow me, but I stick my nose in the air and stride away. If Steph would rather be with these brain-dead idiots, that's her choice.

"Isn't she high and mighty?" a voice yells from behind me.

I ignore it and keep going. Every step feels like I'm dragging a cement brick with me.

"Kat!" Steph cries out. I pause for a moment, struggling to keep myself from turning around. She's my best friend, but she chose Mike. I keep walking and don't look back. Her choice is obvious and so is mine.

Chapter Fifteen

The next morning, Sarah stomps into the kitchen, destroying my solitude. I look up from my bowl of cereal, ready to clear the air between us. There's an empty place inside me after leaving Steph at the dam. I have no energy for another confrontation.

"Hey, you still mad at me?"

Sarah shrugs, flops on the chair and sticks her bottom lip out in a pout. I fight the temptation to snap at her for acting like a spoiled brat.

"Oh, come on – I was only trying to talk to you. You didn't have to take off like that."

"You treat me like a baby. I'm not a baby!"

"You don't have to yell." I hold my breath, waiting to see

if Mom or Dad come running. "I don't treat you like a baby, but you sure act like one sometimes." I ignore Sarah when she sticks her tongue out. "I don't know why I even bother. I was only trying to tell you not to be so affectionate now that you're getting older."

"But it's Uncle Greg. Why can't I hug Uncle Greg?"

I stare into my bowl of cereal. "You just shouldn't. It's not right to do that as you get older – you aren't a baby anymore. You're just too big to be hugging him." How do you explain something like this to a kid like Sarah?

"Why? People always hug and kiss on TV."

"Good morning, girls." Mom walks into the kitchen with her briefcase.

"Mommy," Sarah says, casting a haughty look my way, "why can't I hug Uncle Greg anymore?"

"What?" Mom looks back and forth between us.

"Why can't I hug Daddy, Uncle Greg, and Jared?" Sarah's bottom lip sticks out even farther than before.

"Oh, not this again. Of course you can hug them." Mom raises her eyebrows at me. "They're family, and you can hug them whenever you want."

"Greg's not family!" My spoon bounces off the table and clatters to the floor.

"He's family to us," my mother says firmly.

My chair falls to the floor as I push it back from the table. "He's not family. He's Dad's friend. Being Dad's friend doesn't mean he's family, and it doesn't mean he should be here all the time, or that he's—"

"What is wrong with you, Katrine?" Mom's face is shocked at my outburst. "Amy and Greg are welcome here any time. You always love seeing them. They've done—"

"Oh, forget it! I can't talk to any of you!" I stomp through the kitchen and out the front door with Sarah's smirk and Mom's shock following me like a dark shadow. Why can't they see what Greg is like?

A rusty, blue Mustang pulls into Scott and Steph's driveway across the road. Steph bursts through the front door in blue jeans that seem to be painted on. She climbs into the car without even looking in my direction. Tim hangs out the window and waves at me, a mocking grin on his face. I immediately raise my finger to him and then feel stupid for lowering myself to his level. I kick the curb in frustration then hop around in pain. Once again, I look like an idiot in front of Steph and her new friends. What a great start to the day.

Scott comes out of his front door and meets me at the end of my driveway, raising an eyebrow as I limp in a circle.

"Hey," Scott greets me, "looks like you're having a great day so far." I glare at him. "I figured you would go with Steph. Mom told me she was over here yesterday."

"We *were* on the mend…"

"Uh-oh. Dare I ask?"

"No, you dare not. Let's just say I don't like her new group of friends and leave it at that."

"Wow, you're touchy today. I don't disagree, though." Scott shakes his head and stares after Mike's Mustang. "They're bad news, but you can't tell her anything. Steph has a mind of her own."

"I can't believe she's so blind. Can't you talk to her?"

"I've tried, but we've argued every time."

I sigh and sit down beside Scott on the brick ledge at the bottom of our driveway.

"I haven't seen you much lately."

Scott shrugs. "I've been busy." He looks down the street to see if our bus is coming. "Are you working after school?"

"I don't know. Aunt Sheila is going to call. I have to wait and see what's happening with a patient."

"That sounds serious."

"Yeah, it is. It's actually really sad." I stare at the road, picturing Taylor's tears and frightened eyes.

"A sick kid?"

I hesitate, recalling Steph's reaction yesterday. It still bothers me that she thought something was wrong with Taylor for not telling. What if Scott says the same thing? *There's only one way to find out.*

"No, an abused girl. Her father has been beating her up." I hold my breath, waiting for his reaction.

Scott whistles. "That's brutal. How old is she?"

I release my breath, relieved that he didn't blame Taylor.

"Sarah's age. I felt terrible for her after she told me."

"Wow, she told you something like that? That's heavy stuff."

"Yeah, I guess so."

"Poor kid. That must've been horrible. I can't imagine

what that would be like." I want to throw my arms around Scott and hug him. I should have known he would come through – he's always been a nice guy.

"Yeah," I say noncommittally.

"Too bad we can't do more for kids like that. It's kind of depressing when you think about it. Anybody I know?"

If Scott cares about helpless children, that might include the one inside me. I suddenly feel a little lighter. Maybe it won't be such a bad day after all.

"I can't tell you who she is."

"It'll probably be in the papers soon. You can't beat these small town reporters when they sniff out a story. Child abuse is a big one around here. Who would have thought it would be so close to home?"

Uncomfortable with Scott's observation, I'm relieved to see the bus coming down the road. I don't want to think about the headline possibilities for Taylor or for myself if our stories ever come to light. It's not something I've considered – having such a dirty, horrible story in the paper for everybody to read.

Steph isn't in the cafeteria for lunch period and she doesn't show for any of our classes. I suppose she's joined Mike and his gang, skipping classes and doing whatever they do. If only there was some way to get through to her and show her he isn't worth it.

I run into the house after school, but nobody is around, and there's no note on the table.

The phone rings just as I dump my knapsack in my room.

"Hello?"

"Hi, Kat." My heart jumps at the sound of Aunt Sheila's voice. Scott's words about the newspapers have bothered me all day. I need to know Taylor is okay.

"How's Taylor?" I take my coat off and throw it on the bed.

"She's fine but exhausted. She's been sleeping for the past three hours after all the interviews this morning. We're keeping her here until her grandparents can pick her up. They should be here by tomorrow."

"What about her father?" I ask.

"He definitely has some explaining to do. I don't know if it will go to court or not."

I release my breath in a loud whoosh. "Will it be in the papers?"

Aunt Sheila is quiet on the other end for a moment. "Probably, if it goes to court. Taylor will be protected as a minor, but the whole situation will be difficult. Her father is a principal."

What would the media do to Taylor? I wonder what Mom's reaction will be since she thinks so highly of Mr. Bradford.

"Don't worry," Aunt Sheila continues, "Taylor will be with her grandparents until this is all straightened out. She likely has a long road ahead of her, but at least she's safe now."

"What about her mom?"

"From what I understand, she will go through a series of interviews to determine her capabilities and perspective on the situation and what her intent is toward Taylor and her brother.

It's too soon to say."

A page for Dr. Williams sounds in the background.

"I guess you have to go. Should I come in?"

"Take a break tonight, unless you want to say good-bye to Taylor."

"Okay, I'll probably come and see her later."

"Kat…"

"Yes?"

"Thanks. I don't know how you did it, but you managed what none of us could do. Somehow you reached out to Taylor and got her to open up. I'm so proud of you. If you were here right now, I'd give you a big hug. How'd you do it?"

"I don't know. I guess I just listened to her and understood."

A second page for Dr. Williams is announced in the background.

"Whatever you did – thanks."

"Sure. Bye."

Aunt Sheila's words surprise me and make me feel good. How *did* I do it? I think it was the child inside me that reached out to Taylor. I understood what she was going through. Who knows? Maybe Taylor was simply ready to tell, and I'm the one who was there. She said she always wanted a big sister.

Briefly, I wonder about her brother Darren and his involvement in the whole situation. Was he aware of it? Did he try to help his sister?

Jared would never sit by and let somebody hurt me, or Sarah. I guess that's one of the reasons I was never able to confide in Jared, even though we are very close. He would have been so upset. Jared is big, but Greg is a lot bigger.

Jared got suspended from school when he was in ninth grade for starting a fight. The other boy, Jamie Wilson, was picking on me. He was pushing me around and calling me names, when Jared and some of his friends came upon us. Jared flipped out. Jamie went home with a bloody nose and black eye. Jared went home with a three-day suspension slip and a sore fist.

If Jared was that upset with Jamie Wilson, I can't imagine what he'd do to Greg – if he believed me.

I need to write in my journal. So much has been happening, and I haven't written anything for days. It almost feels like I'm neglecting a part of myself.

I head out the patio door. The backyard is starting to fill with leaves of gold, red, orange, and brown. They rustle and scatter when I walk through them to the clubhouse. The air smells fresh and crisp. An image of Taylor jumping into a pile of leaves lightens my step.

In the clubhouse, everything looks familiar at first glance – the table in the middle with the wooden chairs, the curtains, Jared's sports equipment piled high – but it feels different. The safe feeling I always get when I walk through the door is missing.

Something's not right here.

Then I see the mess behind the table. Skipping ropes, dishes from my old tea set, and Barbie clothes spill from the milk crates that have fallen onto the floor.

I shove the milk crates out of my way and look behind them.

My journal is gone.

Chapter Sixteen

Paralyzed, I stare at the empty spot on the floor. Where's my journal?

Right now, somebody could be reading every word of all the personal things I wrote. If that's so, then somebody knows the truth. I've lost control of my secret.

I panic. *I have to find my journal.*

Dropping to my hands and knees, I root through the mess on the floor, hoping to feel the familiar black book. I toss plates from my tea set across the room and ignore the shattering noise as they break against the walls. There's nothing under the mountain of Barbie clothes either.

Who could have taken it? Nobody knows it's here. My face is wet with tears. *I have to find it. Nobody can read it. It's mine.*

"Hey Kat, you didn't answer your door, so I figured you'd be down here. I need to talk to you about Steph—"

I jerk and my head bashes into the table. Any other time I would have laughed at him, standing speechless in the doorway of the clubhouse with his mouth hanging open.

"Jeez Kat, what's going on?" Scott rushes over and kneels in front of me.

He reaches for my arms, but I pull back, trying to hide my tears.

"I have to find it. I have to!" I don't resist when he pulls me closer, letting me rest my head on his shoulder.

"Okay, we'll find it," he whispers. "What're we looking for?"

"Who could have it? I have to get it back," I sob. "No, no, no – it can't be gone."

"What can I do, Kat? How can I help?" Scott's voice sounds strangled.

Huge sobs rack my body, leaving me fighting for breath.

"Kat, you're scaring the hell out of me. Look at me." Scott's voice is soft, yet firm.

I raise my head. The strength and tenderness in his eyes reach out to me, taking some of the edge off my panic. His arms chase away some of the chill. The only other person who has ever made me feel this safe is Jared.

Scott breaks the silence. "Talk to me, please."

"My – my…My journal is gone."

His lips turn up slightly. "That's it? We'll find it."

"No – no. That's not it."

"Okay. What else?"

I try to gather my thoughts. What can I do? I have no idea where to start. I try to pull away from Scott, but his grip on my arms becomes stronger.

"Trust me, Kat. I'll always be here to help you." Scott lowers his head.

Trust me. Trust me. Scott's words ring inside my head. He's always come through for me when I've really needed him.

But to tell the secret – to share something so dirty and deep and dark – could I do that with Scott?

Who else do you have? Somebody else out there knows.

I pull away and sit back against the wall. Scott sits on the floor, waiting.

"Kat, I know something's wrong. You haven't been yourself lately. I don't know how to help you because you won't talk to me."

"I don't know if I can. Besides, you haven't been around much lately."

"I'm here now. Tell me what's going on." His voice is firm with a touch of impatience.

"You might feel differently toward me." I shiver at the thought of Scott hating me.

"Don't you know I could never feel differently toward you?" Scott sighs, shifts his weight and grabs my hand, sending warm shock waves through my body. I trust his words as if he was Jared.

"It's not pretty."

"I guessed that much." Scott squeezes my hand.

"I have a secret in my journal."

"A secret?"

I watch Scott, needing to look into his eyes and see the expression on his face. So many thoughts and feelings bombard me: the child inside me needs my help, how difficult it is to bear this burden alone, how much Taylor's life will change, the pain of Steph's betrayal and how lonely her absence makes me, and Greg's terrible threats.

Scott squeezes my hand, distracting me from the chaos inside my head.

"About Greg…"

Scott's eyes narrow, but he maintains eye contact. "What about Greg?"

"About what he does to me." The words come out in a soft whisper.

"About what?" Scott asks. Did he not hear my whisper, or does he need me to say the words again?

Tears gather in my eyes. I can say it again.

"The things he does to me." This time, the words startle me with their forcefulness, ringing through the silence in the clubhouse, loud and clear.

Scott's grip tightens as his body tenses. His eyes narrow and the corners of his mouth pull into a frown.

My heart slams against my chest and the ball inside my stomach throbs. I tense in reaction to Scott's body language. Could I have been wrong about him? Should I have trusted him? I want to look away so I don't have to see disgust on Scott's face, but I can't – something inside me won't let me move.

Scott closes his eyes, his heavy breathing filling the silence in the room. The loss of eye contact releases me from my frozen state and I jerk away, ready to get up and run.

Suddenly his eyes snap open. I jump when Scott reaches out and pulls my hand back into his.

Surprisingly, his grip is gentler than it was before.

"Don't pull away from me. Tell me what that bastard did to you."

"I…" I stammer, shocked at Scott's intensity and language. "I…I can't."

"Tell me what he did to hurt you."

Scott's words echo in my head. Scott doesn't think it's my fault. I can do this.

"He touches me…" I say, staring into the brown haven of Scott's eyes, "…and he makes me touch him. He…he does things to me."

Scott's breathing deepens and his lips thin into a straight line.

"I don't want to do those things, Scott. Honest, I don't." The last few words come out in a whimper.

The tears fall from my eyes and track down my cheeks. The words make me feel dirty and cheap. They ring inside me, twisting my heart, as if trying to suffocate it. The world is swimming in a dizzy circle, dragging me down into an endless black hole.

Suddenly, Scott pulls on my hand, jerking me toward him and bringing me out of the dark pit. I'm buried in his arms, unable to move from his iron grip.

We sit, wrapped together, crying and rocking.

Finally, Scott breaks the silence. "I'm sorry, Kat. I didn't know. I should've helped you, but I didn't know."

Suddenly, Scott gasps. "The other night after finding Sarah – he tried to get rid of me so fast – did he—"

I shake my head, fighting the fog enveloping my brain.

"Did it happen again that night because I left? I'm so sorry." A tear falls down Scott's cheek.

"No, nothing happened. Amy came to find him and they went home."

Scott expels a long breath, then his muscles tense again.

"That night when I picked you up after the party, you freaked out. Why?"

Sighing, I look into his eyes. "Scott, you have to understand. I don't sleep much because I have nightmares about him. It was dark, the party was horrible, I was upset, and I fell asleep in the van. Maybe I was dreaming of him, or maybe I just woke up disoriented. I don't know. At first, I thought you were Greg." Scott pulls away, but I grip his arms, determined to make him understand. "You're nothing like him, Scott. I just wasn't myself, and I wasn't thinking straight. I was really out of it."

"You ran from me." Scott brushes his hand over his face, in obvious agitation and hurt.

"Scott, I know you'd never hurt me. I wouldn't be sitting here, confiding in you, otherwise. I've never told anybody."

"How long, Kat? How long have you had to live with this?"

"For as long as I can remember." I stop fidgeting with my hands to brush the tears off my cheeks.

"When we were kids?"

I nod. "I was always the odd one out growing up. Jared was Dad's champion and when Sarah was born, she was his little angel. I couldn't figure out where I fit in. Greg made me feel special and loved." Scott grimaces, while I pause to gather my thoughts. My voice grows stronger as I talk about the things I've never been able to put into words before. "When I started realizing it was wrong, he threatened me. By then I thought it was my fault."

"I'll kill him. I'll find him and kill him for doing this to you." Scott pushes me away and jumps to his feet.

"No!" I scramble to my feet and grab his arm.

"Why are you protecting him? He deserves it for what he did to you." His voice breaks on the last few words.

"I'm not protecting him." I fold my arms across my chest. "I'm protecting myself – and you."

Scott spins to walk away. "I don't need protection, Kat. He's sick, and somebody has to do something."

I grab his arm again, angry that he is taking control of the situation. "No, Scott. You can't make this decision for me. You're being like him and not listening to me."

Scott stops and whispers, "How could you say that?"

"You're taking control and not thinking about how I feel." I let go of his arm as he turns to look at me. Tears run down my cheeks. "I'm not ready, Scott. Mom and Dad wouldn't even believe me. He's been Dad's best friend since high school. They'll blame me."

"You don't know that. They're your parents. Of course they'll believe you. What if he does it again, Kat?" Scott pulls me back into a hug.

"I won't let him." I pull away and look up Scott. "I want to help myself, but I need to do it my way, in my own time."

"If he touches one hair on your head…"

"He won't – not anymore."

Scott puts my head on his shoulder.

"I can't imagine what you've been through." Scott's voice shakes with emotion. "He's so much bigger than you. What if he hits you or something? You need to tell your parents."

"How would he explain bruises to my parents? He's too smart."

I tell Scott about my confrontation with Amy and the lies he told her. I also tell him about my fear of the reporters and newspapers and having everybody know. It would be awful going to school and having everyone look at me, knowing what I did with Greg. It would affect Dad's law practice and Mom's job at school.

"You shouldn't be protecting your parents; they should be protecting you. Please come to me when you need to."

"I can't. He'll hurt you."

"I can protect myself, Kat. Promise you'll come to me."

"I'll try." I say and step away from him. "This is so weird. I feel like I'm dreaming this. I didn't think I would ever be able to tell anybody."

My load really does feel a little lighter. I'm no longer alone.

Looking around at the mess in the clubhouse, I suddenly remember my missing journal.

"Scott – my journal. Everything is in there. I have to find it."

Chapter Seventeen

Sitting on the floor of the clubhouse, I raise my knees and look around, the cold from the wall seeping through my shirt.

Where did I have it last?

I stare at the milk crates where my journal should be. The loss of something so personal and important makes me feel hollow inside.

What's happened in here lately, other than my talk with Scott a few days ago?

I feel warmer when I think about Scott's support. We seem closer again, and I no longer feel like he's avoiding me. In fact, he's been checking on me two or three times a day to see how I'm doing.

I have the feeling I'm missing something. Scott sometimes

seems on the verge of saying something and then stops.

To my surprise, I'm disappointed when he doesn't. What do I want him to say? The whole situation scares and excites me. I wish things were simpler right now. Will I ever be ready for anything else?

I stand up to grab my phone off the table when it rings. "Hello?"

"Hi, it's me."

I smile when I hear Scott's voice. "Hey, I was just thinking about you." Scott doesn't reply. "Scott? Are you still there?"

"Yeah, I'm here. Sorry, you caught me off guard. Good things, I hope?" His voice has a funny catch.

"Of course. You've been keeping me sane the last few days."

"I've got a question for you, and don't say no without thinking about it."

My stomach flip-flops in anticipation. Is he going to finally tell me what's been on his mind? "Okay, shoot." I try to keep my voice light.

"Steph has been asking about you. She's been bugging me to ask you if she can come see you."

I'm suddenly disappointed. What was I expecting? I should be happy that Steph wants to come and talk again.

"Uh…I don't know. She made it pretty clear what her priorities were the last time I saw her."

"She broke up with Mike."

"Oh." Could there be a chance we could patch our friendship? "I don't know…probably…let me think about it."

"Okay. Try to give her a break, Kat. She feels bad, and she's upset."

"Okay, I'll see."

"Are you in the clubhouse again?"

"Yeah, still no luck. I can't figure out where it could be."

"I have to take off for a while. I'll come over and help later."

"Thanks Scott. I'll see you soon."

"Bye."

I set the phone on the table, staring at the empty stack of milk crates. *I know I put it away the last time I wrote in it. Who could have found it? Could Sarah have stolen it? If that little—*

"Hello, Kat."

"Amy…." Has Greg told her more lies? I fidget with my shaking hands, waiting for her to say something.

We stare at each other in silence for a few seconds before she drops a bag on the table. I stare, shocked when my journal slides out of it.

I snatch up the book, holding it against my chest. I feel the sting of betrayal. I love and trust Amy, and she took my journal. "How could you?" I stare at her, still clutching the book to my chest.

"I've been hearing such terrible things. I saw the book when the milk crates fell and I had to know. The things you wrote…are they true?" Amy stares at the journal wrapped in my arms.

I struggle with a storm of emotions. "Does it make any difference what I say?" I glare at Amy.

"No, I suppose it doesn't." Amy shakes her head and begins to pace in the small space of the clubhouse. "How could this happen? I trusted…" Amy pauses and looks directly at me, then looks away again. She raises her voice enough to make me flinch with every word. "I trusted both of you. I did everything for you. You're the daughter I never had." She turns quickly, grabs the journal from me, and throws it against the wall. I jump at the loud thud it makes when it lands beside me. I draw in my breath, smarting from her words. I don't think I could feel more pain if Amy had stabbed me with a knife.

"I guess there's nothing left to say then." I turn away from her, unable to stand looking at the woman who spent more time with me over the last few years than my own mother and father. I can't make her understand. He's her husband, and she loves him. She blames me and why shouldn't she? It's just like he always said it would be.

"I'm sorry," I whisper and start fighting back sobs. "I didn't want to…I didn't want to betray you…I'm so sorry." I pick up the journal and shelter it in my arms, trying to breathe between sobs. *I'm going to lose everyone I love. I don't deserve their love.*

"Kat—" I feel Amy's touch on my shoulder, but when I turn around she pulls away, as if burned, tears on her cheeks. My body jerks with sobs as Amy tilts her head to look at me.

"You're so young still," she whispers.

Staring at the floor in shame, I hear Amy start to move away from me. There's a sudden pause in her movement and then a loud smack. I look up as she winds up for a second kick to the doorframe of the clubhouse. "How could he do this to me? How could he? I'm such a fool!" We both stand without saying a word for what seems like hours. The only sound is the intake of our breaths between sobs.

"Amy, I…"

She lifts her head and looks at me. I've never seen such devastation on anybody's face. She doesn't even look like Amy. She puts her hand out like a barrier, shaking her head.

"I don't want to hear it, Kat. I've read it, and I don't know what to say. I wasn't even going to come. At first, I was just going to ignore it. Stupid me, thinking it would just go away." I hold my breath. She looks at me and shakes her head. "It won't go away, though. You're here and will always be here to remind me. Why did you have to be here to tempt him?" Her voice grows louder as she speaks the last few words.

Shame, anger, and hurt clog my throat, leaving me speechless and in shock.

Amy stares out of sightless eyes and begins speaking as if I'm not there. "I know I can't ignore it. How am I supposed to look at him, talk to him, or even look at you?" She kicks the doorframe again, this time with much less enthusiasm than the last few kicks. "I know…" Amy stops for a moment, sighing. "I'm probably not being fair to you right now, but this isn't fair to me, either." Her last few words are barely a whisper.

"Amy, please let me…"

"No, Kat. I knew what I was doing when I came here but wouldn't admit it. Good-bye, Kat."

I swallow past the lump in my throat, and clutch the journal even tighter to remind myself this is real, not a dream.

Things are about to change forever.

"What...what do you mean?"

Amy's stance straightens slightly as a look of resignation floods her face. "I need to get away and think. I need some time. I can't face him – or you – right now."

I'm suddenly consumed by a burning need to know if Greg was right or not. "Do you...do you believe me?" I whisper.

"I don't know," Amy shakes her head. "Maybe that's not true. How can all of that be a lie?" Amy's voice catches as she looks at the journal. "If I accept this, it means he played me for a total fool." Her voice rises with her anger again. She suddenly turns, fidgets with her finger, and throws her wedding ring onto the table. It bounces a few times with the force and lands in the corner where my name is carved. We both stare at it for a moment, and then Amy laughs bitterly. "He played all of us. And the things that happened in – well, they just don't seem possible." We stare at each other, thick tension separating us. "It means I married a man who is still a stranger." Amy clenches her fists and starts pacing again. "The man I read about in your journal isn't the one I know. What am I supposed to do?"

Amy's question hangs in the air. We both know there is no answer.

"Will you come back?" My heart hammers in my chest, waiting. I'm starting to feel faint and fight to stay on my feet. Why do I feel like the one responsible for her leaving? It's not all my fault!

"I don't know." Amy wipes a tear from her cheek.

I catch a glimpse of something red out of the corner of my eye. It's Sarah's red coat, and she's standing just outside the door of the clubhouse. Tears run down her cheeks and her hand covers her mouth.

"No! You can't leave. Don't let Kat make you leave."

I walk toward Sarah. "Sarah—"

"No! You stay away from me." Sarah points at me, backing out the door. "You're making Amy leave." She turns and runs toward the bush.

A dead weight settles inside me at the thought of never seeing Amy again and handling another episode with Dad because Sarah has disappeared for the second time in a week. Why did she have to show up now?

"Bye, Kat. If I see Sarah I'll talk to her. I just need to get out of here."

"I'm sorry, Amy." I'm not even sure if she hears my whisper at first, but then she pauses on her way to the door, and we stare at each other for a moment. It looks as if she is about to say something, but then she leaves.

I struggle to comprehend that I'm losing Amy. *Thanks to him!*

She walks away from me, in the same direction Sarah disappeared into the bush. I sink to the floor, drawing my knees to my chest and cover my face with my hands. The journal falls beside me.

Amy was like a second mother, spending time with me, taking me places, and being here for me to confide in when I felt uncomfortable going to my own mother. Now she's gone.

If I were a stronger person, this wouldn't be happening. I would never have let him touch me.

I sit like this for a long time, my legs stiffening, but unable to move.

"Hello, Kitty Kat."

I freeze at the sound of his voice.

Chapter Eighteen

I grip strands of my hair, fighting the urge to look at him. I can feel his cold eyes staring through me. I know he's probably standing there, arms crossed over his chest with a smirk on his face. Flames of impatience and anger usually spark in his eyes when his voice takes on this tone. I've seen that look a thousand times.

Did he see Amy leave? Is that why he's angry?

"Wh-what...do you want, Greg?" My hands are still covering my head, hiding me as if I were a frightened puppy. I struggle with the urge to scream at him. *Don't do it, Kat. He'd be furious. Just sit here and maybe he'll go away. Go away, Greg. Go away.* I rock back and forth in rhythm with the words going through my head.

"Tsk, tsk, tsk, Kat. You know what I want and you haven't been cooperating." Greg's voice slips into the soft, coaxing mode that he uses when he wants something.

Please just leave me alone. Leave.

His steps signal my doom as he approaches, and I'm nauseated by the familiar smell of his cologne. It's quiet except the sound of our heavy breathing. I peek under my arms and see him looking into the corner. Picking up Amy's ring up from the floor, he stares at it, turning it in his fingers.

I push up against the wall as much as I can and hide my head deeper within the shelter of my arms. His steps come closer, heavy and determined, and he touches my arm. My skin crawls and a lump lodges in my throat, choking any protests.

"Where's my wife?" Greg's voice is soft and soothing, as if coaxing a baby to sleep.

"I…I don't know." I rock, trying to break contact with him.

His grip tightens, preventing my rocking. "Don't lie to me, Kitty Kat. You know I don't like that. What is her ring doing here?" His voice grows louder and angrier with every word.

Silence falls between us.

"I stopped to drop some papers off, but nobody answered the door. And now, I come down here and find this. Where's Amy, Kat? Tell me now!" He shakes my arm in frustration.

I remain silent, my head still on my knees, my fingers tangled in my hair, trying to keep my face down and hidden. I'm shaking like a leaf from the force of his anger. *Don't say anything. Don't say anything.*

"What did you tell her?"

I jump and wince when he squeezes my arm hard and jerks it away from my head, causing me to pull out the strands of hair that were wrapped around my fingers. My heart pounds and my body tenses until my muscles burn.

Greg yanks me so violently to my feet that pain shoots all the way to my shoulder. He grips my chin and tips my head up to look at him. Power radiates from this towering, red-faced beast standing in front of me, dwarfing me. The cold clubhouse wall at my back has me trapped.

"N-n-n-nothing."

He lets go of my chin and clenches my other arm to lift me so I dangle above the ground. "Don't lie to me," he says, emphasizing each word. "You know what happens when you're disobedient, Kitty Kat."

Please, no. I shake uncontrollably.

Greg smirks, thinking he's won. "That's my girl. Now, tell me what you said to Amy."

Resentment boils through my veins. I hate him. A red haze forms before my eyes. I hate his smirk. I hate his tone of voice. I hate his hands. I hate his power and his ability to control everything. My fists clench at my sides, itching to make contact with his face so I can scratch his eyes out.

Greg drops me, leaving me to struggle for balance.

"It doesn't matter. She's always going to take my word over yours. I'm the perfect husband; she'd have no reason to believe anything you'd say to her."

Do I detect uncertainty in his voice?

"She *depends* on me and *needs* me." Greg starts to sound more confident once again, as he slips the ring in his pocket. "I'll find Amy and fix whatever you told her. I'm always fixing your messes, Kat." Greg touches my arms again, this time lightly rubbing his fingers up and down. I'm thankful for the cool weather and the bulky sweatshirt I'm wearing.

"Right now, I think you owe me an apology, Kitty Kat." Greg's voice turns soft and husky. This is the voice I hate the most. This is the voice that haunts my dreams.

Greg moves his hand to caress my cheek. "Come on, I don't like to stay mad at you." His hands are behind me, pressing up and down my body, pushing me closer to him. His breath on my cheek becomes heavier, sending waves of revulsion through me.

I look away, trying to find the courage to put an end to this, but I can feel myself regressing into the disobedient little girl inside, prepared to take my punishment.

My eyes dart around the clubhouse, searching for a focal point to distract myself from his hands. This was the only place I could come and escape from Greg – a place he'd never been in – until today. As if he hasn't stolen enough from me, now he's stolen my only haven.

I struggle to block his musky scent by studying the signatures on the wooden table. I spy my journal out of the corner of my eye, a blinding reminder of everything that this man has put me through.

Resentment flashes again. I remember Amy's tears and the horrible emptiness I felt when she said she would probably never return. And then there's Scott. He didn't blame me for this. He said he would stand by me and always be there – and I promised never to let Greg touch me again.

Scott trusted me and supported me, and I made him a promise. I made myself a promise!

I shiver when Greg lifts my shirt and touches my skin, exposing me to the cool air in the clubhouse. *Can I stop him?*

"No, stop!" I push against Greg's chest. It's like trying to budge a mountain.

Greg ignores my plea and my shove. He's so arrogant and sure that he can control everyone in his life.

No more! He's not going to control me anymore!

With a burst of adrenaline, I draw in a huge breath and push at Greg's chest, knocking us both off balance. I scramble away from the wall, toward the door of the clubhouse.

Greg recovers quicker than I thought he would and grabs my arm.

"Come on, Kat…please."

For once, I feel no guilt. I don't owe him a thing.

"No. I don't want you to touch me."

"Okay, Kat. You're upset. It's okay. I even forgive you for whatever you told Amy. I know I can fix it for you."

Shaking my head, I try to pull away, but he still has a hold on me.

"Come here." Greg's voice is more firm now, but I continue to pull away. In desperation, I sink my fingernails into his arm.

"You little—" Greg explodes, his face turning red.

We both freeze when my dad shouts Greg's name. I can see Dad through the clubhouse door, standing on the lawn, shading his eyes from the sun.

For the very first time I can see a flicker of uncertainty in Greg's eyes.

Chapter Nineteen

Greg's uncertainty stokes my courage, replacing the cold emptiness that has been my constant companion. It chases away my fear. It dawns on me that I have the upper hand.

"Down here, Dad." My eyes remain fixed on Greg.

"Kat, is Greg with you? His car is in the driveway."

Greg's eyes narrow in silent warning. *He wants me to tell Dad that he's not in here.* Squaring my shoulders, I stand tall; I will not lie for him anymore.

I smile at Greg, enjoying the freedom from his control. But when I turn to leave the clubhouse, my arm is wrenched back. My head jerks violently, and my teeth snap together. Greg's fingers are like a band of steel around my arm. He thrusts me behind him, and leaves the clubhouse, without looking back.

From the window, I watch Dad walk down to meet Greg and clap him on the shoulder. Their voices drift toward me.

"What were you doing down here?"

"I was just chatting with Kat. I stopped by to drop off the papers."

"The trip was a success?" Dad turns with Greg to walk toward the house.

Forcing my feet to move, I follow them.

"It was. I have the information in my car. I'll get it." Greg glances over his shoulder, narrowing his eyes when he sees me following. Turning back to Dad, he says, "Better yet, let's go for a drink to celebrate."

"No, that's okay. You've been gone a few days. Leave the papers with me, and go home to Amy. "

"She's not there," I blurt out, without thinking.

Dad looks back at me.

"Was her car in the driveway when you got home?" I ask Dad, ignoring Greg's glare.

"No. Why?"

"She was here to say—"

Greg steps in front of Dad, blocking our eye contact. "Come on, David, let's get that drink. I'll track Amy down later. I have a lot to tell you, and I'd rather finish our business before going home."

Dad turns to walk to the house with Greg. *Am I ready to tell him?* Watching Dad walk away with Greg is hard to swallow. The frustration of defeat overwhelms me; I can't do this in front of Greg.

This is your only chance. Snap out of it! Don't blow it!

The image of Amy leaving fuels me. Greg has ruined so many lives, hurt so many people. I want him to suffer. I want him to hurt so much more than all the suffering he has caused.

A shout draws our attention to the corner of the house as Scott barrels around the corner, shouting my name over and over. We all stand, shocked, until it suddenly dawns on me that this can't be good. I step forward and yell at him to stop, but I'm too late.

"You son of a—" Scott's outburst is cut off as he launches through the air and tackles Greg to the ground.

Greg recovers quickly and throws Scott off. Dad grabs Scott from behind and holds him as he scrambles to get up and attack again.

"What's wrong with you?" Dad yells, jerking Scott back as he lunges again.

This can't be happening. Please make this stop. Please let this all be a dream.

Mom steps through the patio doors. "What's going on? I heard shouting." She shivers in the cool air, rubbing her hands up and down her arms. "David, why are you holding onto Scott?"

I glance from Mom to Dad. *Will they believe me? What if I never feel this strong again? I have to say something before Scott does.*

I shake my head back and forth. *No! No, no, no, no, this can't be happening!*

"Kat, what is it? What's going on here?" My mom leaves the porch and hurries across the backyard. I look around and realize they are all staring at me. I must have cried out loud.

Greg recovers faster than I do. "I'm sure this is a big misunderstanding. David, why don't we…"

"No!" Scott yells and jerks toward him again, but Dad manages to hold on to him. "You know damn well there's no misunderstanding. You're sick. You belong—"

This is your only chance. Take control. I'm tired of being afraid and thinking I'm the bad one. I'm tired of being his victim. I'm tired of not fighting for myself.

"Scott, stop it. Stop it, now. This is my decision!" I stare into his blazing eyes until he stops struggling. Dad's arms relax, but he doesn't let go.

"Kat, what's this all about?" Dad demands to know.

Out of the corner of my eye, I see Greg turn toward me. I can feel the anger radiate from him, even from where I stand. I focus on Dad and Scott, my heart beating furiously.

"Amy is gone." *Did I just say that?* "She couldn't stand to see him again." I point to Greg. The words tumble from my mouth.

Mom gasps, and Dad stares at me, as if trying to decide whether he should believe me or not.

"Do you know what she's talking about?" he turns toward Greg.

Greg chuckles and shrugs. "No idea, David. I talked to Amy on my cell just before I got here."

He did not *talk to Amy. Amy was here, and Greg was looking for her. It's just one more nasty, disgusting lie to add to the pile that he started when I was a child.*

"Kat, why would you say something like that?" Mom stares at me with shocked eyes.

Scott begins to struggle again, glaring at Greg. "You snake!"

My worst fear crashes down on me – my parents take Greg's word over mine. I would expect this from Dad, but I had always hoped Mom would stand by me.

My head buzzes and I try to fight all the second thoughts warring inside me. I don't want to think. I don't want to see him. I don't want him to win. I want my parents to love me.

"He's lying." I point toward Greg, unable to control the words tumbling out. "He's been lying for years. Amy found out, and that's why she left."

"Kat, that's enough." My father's authoritative voice seems to waver slightly.

I pace back and forth. "No, it's not enough. He's lying to you. He lies to me. He told me that I have to prove I love him…and that he loves me…and that I'm his special girl."

I stop pacing and plead with my eyes, desperate for my parents to understand and forgive me. Dad releases Scott abruptly. Scott stumbles from straining against the grip that suddenly isn't there anymore.

"He told me that I was a good girl if I did it, and that nobody would love me if I told. He told me it was my fault. He lied when he said that it's okay for him to touch me. I was younger than Sarah is now that first time. I believed everything."

I choke on my sobs, no longer able to continue. I'm so tired. I collapse to my knees, covering my face with my hands. The emotions I've been holding in for so long pour out, like poison flowing from an open wound. A high-pitched screech escapes, releasing the pain and frustration that has been building for years.

The echo of my scream dies away, and I raise my head to the tense silence surrounding us. Mom's eyes are wide with shock. Dad's mouth is open, his fists clenched at his sides. Greg is standing with his eyes closed. His smirk is gone.

We are all frozen in time – statues – until Dad grabs Greg's shirt collar.

"You son of a bitch, what did you do to my daughter? What's she talking about?"

"Come on, David. I'd never do anything to hurt her. Your family is my family, remember?"

"No, my family is *my* family!" Dad's face is red and his eyes bulge.

Mom rushes over and pulls his arm. "David, let him go."

Dad glares at Mom. "Get back, Maria." He uses his free hand to push her behind him. Scott takes her by the arm and moves her farther away from Dad and Greg.

"Where the hell did you touch my daughter? What did you do?"

"Oh, get real, David. Look at her. She's a kid. What would I want with a kid when I have Amy? She's lying." Greg looks at me, a sneer on his lips. "She's had a crush on me. I haven't said anything because I thought I could handle it myself. She has even been trying to blackmail me. Amy knows all this. Let go and we'll talk about it. We can work it out and get Kat the help she needs."

I draw in a deep breath and wait for Dad's inevitable look of condemnation. Mentally I prepare for Dad's response, sure that he will turn on me for saying such horrible things about his best friend. How will I ever face him again if he believes Greg's lies?

Fight for yourself, Kat. Take control.

Releasing my breath, I rise from my knees and walk toward Greg and my father.

My steps falter for a moment when Scott walks toward me, but I manage to keep going. Scott reaches for my hand. His silent show of support stokes my determination.

I hold his hand but look toward my father and stare directly into his eyes. "If you think I'd lie about something like *this*, you don't know me, and I'm not your daughter."

Dad gazes at me in stunned silence.

Chapter Twenty

Greg's shirt collar is still gathered in Dad's fist, but both of them seem frozen.

"Daddy," I finally whisper, unable to stand his silence any longer. I can hear Mom sobbing behind me. A tear falls from my father's eye – something I've never seen before – and trickles down his stubbled cheek. I almost expect it to disappear into the recesses of my imagination.

As if sensing how much trouble he may be in, Greg struggles against Dad's hold on his shirt. The rest happens so fast, I can't even say who threw the first punch. Within seconds, Dad and Greg are engulfed in a vicious struggle, the sound of their grunts and punches ringing through the air.

Scott drags me away from the swinging fists to where Mom is. I stand, numb, with Scott holding one hand and Mom the other.

Greg loses his balance when Dad swings at him again. Greg falls to the ground and pulls Dad's arm, taking him down as well. They continue their battle, rolling around on the damp grass.

A flash of red comes into view down by the woods. I hold my breath, hoping to see Amy following behind Sarah, but she doesn't appear.

"Mommy, make them stop!" Sarah yells, flying toward my mom and hugging her around the waist. Sarah's sobs are muffled in my mom's skirt.

Another loud crack draws my attention back to the fight. Dad's face swings to the side, an arc of blood following the motion of his head.

"This has to stop." Mom disentangles herself from Sarah and runs across the lawn, disappearing through the patio doors. Sarah follows close behind, still crying.

What if Greg really hurts Dad? It will be my fault. I never imagined that this would happen and I'd be standing here watching them try to tear each other apart.

I approach them, trying to find a way to break up the fight. Now Greg is on top of Dad. I grab his jacket, trying to pull him off. "Leave him alone."

Greg swings his arm around, knocking me in the face and sending me to the ground. "Get away, you little…"

I huddle on the ground, covering my bloody nose. Dad

throws Greg off him. "Don't you ever touch my daughter or anybody in my family again."

Scott grabs my arm, pulling me up and farther away from the scuffle.

"That's enough. I've called the police. Break it up – now!"

I hadn't even heard or seen Mom come back out from the house. The fact that she has called the police begins to register in my muddled brain.

What will happen to everyone? What will happen to me? Will my parents tell them what Greg has been doing to me?

"Kat, what happened?" Mom is staring at me with wide eyes. She gently touches my cheek where Greg hit me. A strange, croaking sound escapes her, and I leave Scott's protection to be enfolded in my mother's arms. How long have I wished for a hug like this?

"You're bleeding. What happened to you?"

"I'm okay, Mom. I got too close. It's just a nosebleed."

"Why are they fighting? Why won't they stop?" Sarah is behind Mom, clinging to her.

"Come here, Sweetie." Mom reaches behind and draws Sarah to her side, still keeping me safe in her other arm. It feels so good to be held like this.

Mom's hands run through Sarah's hair, trying to calm her.

I didn't want it to happen this way. I feel Mom tremble when Greg's fist makes contact with Dad's cheek. I never should have said anything. This is my fault.

The wail of the police sirens draws closer.

"Are they going to take Daddy away?" Sarah whispers.

Mom's eyes look sad. Squeezing both of us, she whispers, "I don't know. I just don't know, Honey." Mom looks into my eyes. "I just don't seem to know much of anything these days."

"I'm sorry, Mom. I didn't mean for this to happen. I'm so sorry." I bury my face in her shoulder, no longer able to stand the sounds of the fight.

Mom's hand feels warm and comforting when it rubs up and down my back. "Don't you be sorry, Kat. We're sorry."

What does she mean? Why is she saying sorry? I'm the one who's screwed everything up.

Sirens and slamming car doors echo from the front yard.

Moments later, two police officers in full uniform run around the side of the house. They rush past us and approach Greg and Dad, who are still rolling around on the ground.

The tall officer drags Dad off Greg and pulls him off to the side. Greg stumbles to his feet to follow, obviously not ready to stop. The other officer immediately moves in and grabs Greg's arms, forcing them behind him. With an ominous click, the cuffs close around Greg's wrists.

Greg struggles with the officer. "What the hell is going on? Let me go." His eyes show signs of desperation.

The officer moves to grab Dad's arms, but Dad holds up his hand. "It's okay. I'm done." The officer nods, but still puts the handcuffs on.

Dad lowers his head to swipe the blood from his lip onto his shoulder, where it leaves a red smear on his ripped shirt. His pants, once a tan color, are covered with grass stains and mud. I've never seen my dad so dishevelled. His hair is sticking straight up, with dead leaves tangled in it. His eye is already starting to bruise and swell, and blood is still running down his nose.

Mom holds Sarah and me close. A shudder runs through her. "David," she whimpers, staring at Dad.

Sarah's sobs pierce the air with renewed volume.

Dad looks at us, as if realizing for the first time that we're standing there. "It's okay, Maria." His voice is familiar and firm, and strangely reassuring.

He looks at Sarah briefly and then locks eyes with me, grimacing in pain as he shifts his weight. For the first time in a long time, I find myself feeling sorry for Dad and wishing I wasn't the cause of his distress.

"It's going to be all right, Kat. We'll work this out," Dad says, before the officer leads him to the front. The other officer follows, pushing Greg, still struggling against the handcuffs, along in front of him.

Emotions bombard me as Greg is taken into custody: fear of what's going to happen next, sadness for everything ending this way, relief and trepidation that my dreadful secret is finally out in the open. Yet, through all of this, the comfort of Dad's parting words echo inside me, controlling my trembling and calming me.

My head pounds and I'm suddenly exhausted. I want to climb into a black hole and forget everything that's happened within the last twenty minutes.

"Kat! Kat, where are you? Kat!" Steph's panicked voice rings out.

"Back here," I whisper, unable to summon the energy to shout any louder.

The tall police officer who pulled Dad off Greg comes back around the house.

"Mrs. Thompson, you made the call?" My mom nods.

"I'm going to have to ask you some questions," he says, stopping in front of the three of us.

Mom moves slightly in front of me, as if sheltering me from the officer's view. She nods and points toward the side of the house. "Let's talk over there."

Scott is immediately by my side and wraps his warm, protective arms around me. I'm no longer angry that he started all of this. I just want to stay sheltered forever.

"Kat!" Steph comes around the corner of the house. She stops a few feet from Scott and me, trying to catch her breath, her eyes swing between us and Mom, walking up the lawn with the officer, followed by Sarah.

Scott cradles my cheeks with both hands and looks into my eyes.

"Are you okay?" He looks relieved when I nod. "Did he hurt you before I got here?" I shake my head and flinch when his hand rubs the tender spot where Greg hit me.

"Who? What's going on?" Steph was never able to wait patiently. Her head swivels back and forth in obvious confusion.

She's here now, but we've lost some of the closeness we once shared. We used to tell each other pretty much everything. Why am I hesitating now?

Sensing my reluctance, Scott turns to his sister. "Why don't you help Mrs. Thompson with Sarah, Steph? It looks like she could use it."

After one last look, as if to let me know that it isn't over, Steph walks over to coax Sarah away from my mom and the officer.

Now that some of the shock of what's happened is fading, I look up at Scott again. "How could you? I told you that it was my decision."

"I know. I'm sorry, Kat. I saw Greg's car and I just…well, I just snapped. I'm sorry."

Sighing, I nod. It's done and there's no going back, even if I wanted to.

Chapter Twenty-One

"Are you sure, Kat? You don't have to do this." Scott glances at me, his concern evident.

Sinking back into the patio chair, I stare blindly, trying to gather my thoughts. Why do things have to be so complicated? Every time I think I've made up my mind, I change it again. Everything happened so fast.

Mom is still with the officer and they have walked around to the front of the house. Steph has taken Sarah inside to try and calm her down.

For what seems like the hundredth time since the craziness began, I've wondered if I'm ready. I feel incapable of making a decision and sticking to it.

"I don't know," I finally whisper.

"Don't rush this, Kat. If you talk to them…well, you have to be sure."

"I think I'm going to see how it feels when we get to the station. I know Mom will go there as soon as the officer leaves, and I want to go along. If I don't say anything, what will they do to Dad?" My stomach tightens with nerves.

"I don't know. But if you say something now, you can't turn back. You have to do it for yourself, not to help your dad out of this mess. He's a big boy – he can handle what's coming. I'm sure he wouldn't expect you to say anything if you're not ready."

"You don't know my father."

"Maybe, but he might surprise you, Kat."

Reluctantly, I admit to myself that Dad has surprised me already. I expected him to turn and yell at me earlier tonight, but he attacked his best friend instead.

Does that mean Dad believes me?

Scott squeezes my hand. I stare at the cold, brick walls of the house, picturing Dad and Greg sitting in prison cells. Would they put them into cells? How would it feel to be behind bars? What is Greg telling the police? A small part of me wishes things could go back to the way they were. I fight the urge to run into the house and try to forget it all happened, but deep down, I know that if I let myself down now, I'll never have the courage to come this far again. *I'll never forgive myself if I don't follow through.*

I see an image of Dad's face as he looked at me just before the officer led him away. He told me that things would work out. Was that the lawyer in him or the father talking?

And then I see Greg, his eyes burning into mine, his lips set in a grim line and his fists clenched in the cuffs behind his back. I focus on this picture, trying to figure out what's missing. He's been angry and upset with me before, he's been sweet and cajoling, he's been domineering, but he's never had a look of hatred like that. That look of hatred on his face made me feel – I stopped dead in my tracks. *GADS!* I didn't feel anything at all! *I wasn't scared of him.*

"Oh, wow," I say, barely realizing that I'm speaking out loud.

"What is it?" Scott leans forward.

"I wasn't scared of Greg. I didn't turn to ice inside like I always have before. What does that mean?" I ask Scott.

"I don't know, Kat. Maybe it means you finally felt safe."

"Yeah, maybe. I always pictured Mom and Dad freaking out – but on me, not Greg. I figured they'd call me a liar for the rest of my life, but they didn't. Even Steph came after everything we've been through lately. I had the courage to speak out and you were all there for me and no one called me a liar. Even Sarah didn't defend Greg this time." I grasp Scott's hand and turn sideways in my seat to look directly at him.

"I had the upper hand!"

A sense of power sweeps over me. It feels so sweet I can almost taste it. *Is this how Greg felt when he had power over me all those years? Did he feel invincible?*

"I can do this, Scott."

Scott studies me for a moment, smiles, and nods.

Chapter Twenty-Two

He's in there, behind bars, and I'm out here. I have the power to keep him there, where he belongs – if I can do this.

I hesitate in front of the doors of the police station. Mom pauses beside me with her hand resting lightly on my shoulder. "You're sure?"

She's asked the same question several times since she finished with the officer at the house and saw the look on my face when she returned to the backyard to find me. It's like she read my mind and knew what I was going to do without asking. I have no idea what explanation she gave the police officer for Dad and Greg's fight, but she didn't tell him about my accusation. I guess she figured it was up to me to decide if I wanted to take it further. Mom was clearly in a state of shock after the officer left. I've never seen her so pale and withdrawn before.

I look at her reflection in the glass door of the station and nod. I'm sure. I think of little Taylor, lying alone in the hospital, with no support from anyone. If she could find the courage to tell, so can I.

Inside, no one is manning the counter, so Mom and I wait. The entrance is pretty much what I expected. The walls are cold and white, and the floor is a dull gray with black scuff marks and smudges. A poster hanging to my right promotes Neighborhood Watch programs and another one advertises an upcoming charity auction to raise money for the homeless. I half expect to see WANTED posters, but aside from pictures of missing children, there are none.

Stacks of pamphlets sit on the counter for people to read. I bend over to pick up one that's fallen to the floor. I reach to return it to the pile, when the bright red words across the top catch my attention. "What Should You Do If You Suspect Child Abuse?" A little girl holding a teddy bear and sucking her thumb is pictured on the front.

I freeze, staring at the words, as they register and repeat in my head. *Child abuse…child abuse…child abuse.* I'm an abused child. Putting a label to me – to something that happened to me – makes it seem so real. I'm a statistic. I'm one of them… one of those numbers mentioned in a pamphlet that someone dropped on the floor not caring enough to pick it up let alone take it home.

"Can I help you?"

I come to attention with a start. Across the counter from

me is a pair of impatient brown eyes, set in the face of a young officer who seems busy and about to rush off again. Fiddling with the pamphlet in my hand, I'm unable to make my brain connect to my mouth. *Say something, Kat. Don't just stare at him. Do you want to be a victim all your life?*

"You okay?" the officer asks, narrowing his eyes and probably wondering what kind of drugs I'm on.

"I…I need to…" I stammer.

"We need to talk to someone." My mom steps in just as another officer walks into the room. I immediately recognize him as the man who pulled Dad and Greg apart at our house.

"It's all right, Chambers, I've got this," he says, and the brown-eyed officer rushes away, a pile of papers under his arm and a look of relief on his face.

"Your name's Kat, isn't it?" The officer waits for me to find my tongue.

I nod stupidly.

"Are you here to add something to your statement?" He glances at Mom.

Mom grips my shoulders with reassuring hands. "Yes, we need to talk to you." She glances around. "If we could go somewhere private—"

"Maria! Don't say a word. I'll handle this." My father comes out through a door to the side. He doesn't look much better than he did when he was taken away, except that the blood has stopped flowing from his nose. His right eye is swollen, he has a fat lip, and a rainbow of blues, purples and blacks colors his face.

"Where's Sarah?"

Mom answers quietly. "She's at home with Steph and Scott. Kat thought maybe she'd like to come and talk to somebody." Mom squeezes my hand, trying to send me a message. I hesitate, uncertain if she is encouraging me to proceed or to listen to Dad. I'm so used to her being a buffer between us that I'm not sure what she is trying to tell me.

"Kat doesn't need to talk to anybody. I'll handle everything."

They're talking about me as if I'm not even here, just like Dad has always done. Talking about me and making all my decisions for me, without even stopping to wonder what I want and think. Years of hearing Dad saying "Kat needs this…" or "Kat doesn't want that…" or "Kat is going to do this…" or, worst of all, "Kat will try better next time…."

No more.

"No," I whisper. Dad looks at me curiously. Mom's eyes are full of fear, but I'm sure I also see a hint of encouragement. The officer raises his eyebrow as if inquiring whether I have more to say.

"No, you won't handle this. I need to talk to somebody." A force rings in my voice that I have never used with Dad.

"Okay, why don't you come this way?" the officer says, walking toward a door marked authorized personnel only.

Dad has found his voice again. "I'll come with her."

Telling a stranger what Greg did to me is one thing, but saying those things in front of my father is another. In time, I might be able to, but not now. Not with the questions they'll ask. How can I admit in front of them the things I let Greg do and the things he made me do to him? I still have a hard enough time admitting them to myself.

"I...I don't think that's a good idea." I hope my father will let it rest this one time and treat me like I'm not a small child.

Dad steps forward, his mouth open in protest, when Mom interrupts and volunteers to come.

Part of me wants Mom there. Part of me wants to cling to her warmth and strength and lose myself in her protection. Will I be able to do this if I have her there? Will I be able to say the things I need to say with her beside me? She hasn't let me down yet, but I might let myself down if she's there. No. I need to do this by myself. I need to fight my demons and say the words.

I shake my head at Mom, begging her with my eyes to understand and not be hurt by my rejection. She smiles sadly and nods.

I follow the officer through the door, down a long beige hallway to a room with a large mirror, a table and four chairs. If I wasn't so nervous I'd probably laugh – it's just what I would picture in the movies.

The officer, following the direction of my stare, shrugs self-consciously. "I know.... Seems like something out of the movies when they're interviewing a murder suspect. We're renovating and we don't have many empty rooms right now. Trust me, there's no one behind the mirror."

I shrug, beginning to wonder if this is all a big mistake.

"Let me just go find the detective. I'll be right back."

"A detective? Why?"

The officer shrugs and looks at me closely. "I think it would be a good idea." He turns and shuts the door behind him.

A murder suspect the cop had said…in a way, it's true. Greg murdered the little girl I used to be. He killed that child the first time he touched me.

Voices interrupt my thoughts and a woman follows the tall officer back into the room.

"I don't know if you remember, but I'm Officer Jackson," the man says, "and this is Detective Donaldson. She's going to talk to you today. We have equipment in this room that will record what you are going to tell us. Do you understand?"

"Yes," I say, barely louder than a whisper.

"We should also let you know that we could do this at the Domestic Violence Unit instead of here, where there are case workers available. Would you like to continue, or would you rather go there?"

"Let's just do it," I say.

Officer Jackson nods and moves out of my direct line of vision to lean against the wall. Detective Donaldson sits across from me at the table. She looks very young. Her blonde hair is pulled back in a bun and her smile seems kind and gentle. She isn't dressed in a police uniform like Officer Jackson. She's wearing blue jeans and a blazer jacket. Her eyes are hard to read, but I can see the lines of fatigue around them.

"Sorry about the room, Kat. I know it's not very comfortable, but it's all we have at the moment," Detective Donaldson says. "Officer Jackson tells me you're looking for somebody to talk to. I understand you had some excitement at your house earlier, and your mother was quite agitated about it. Is this what you want to talk about?"

I nod and stare at the diamond ring on her hand. She must have somebody at home waiting for her, somebody who cares about her, no matter what happens.

"Do you want to talk about your dad?" she asks.

The light sparkles off the diamond when she turns her hand. Unable to lift my eyes, I shake my head.

"Okay. Is this about another family member?"

Again, I shake my head, still unable to look into her eyes, afraid she'll be able to read everything that's going on inside me.

"Officer Jackson told me the man fighting with your father is a family friend. Is it him you want to talk about?"

Fidgeting with my hands, I wonder what a diamond like that would look like on my finger. Would it feel cold or warm? Would it protect me from all evil? Could I have used it to scratch Greg's eyes out when he came near me?

"Kat?"

I remain silent for a few more moments before I hear her soft voice again. "Would you like to try this again another day?"

Chapter Twenty-Three

Come back again? If I walk out of this station right now, I'll never come back.

I raise my head and look into the detective's eyes. Is it my imagination, or is there understanding there?

"No, I don't want to come back. I want to do this now."

"All right then. Let's go. Are you ready?"

I nod and inhale a deep breath of stale air. "I want to talk about Greg."

"Greg is the man your father fought with? He's a friend of your father's?"

"Yes, since high school."

"You've known Greg for a long time?"

"All my life."

"Are you and Greg close?"

Close is one word you could use. I start fidgeting with my hands, trying to spit out the words that are lodged tight in my throat.

"Did something about that question upset you, Kat?"

I didn't think it would be this hard saying the words to a stranger. I look around the room, my eyes resting briefly on Officer Johnson, who is standing in the corner. My palms are wet and clammy while I fidget with them. I try to think and ignore the ringing in my ears.

"I…, um…I'd like my mom to come in."

"Would you like me to get her?" Officer Johnson asks.

"Yes…. I mean, no. No, it's okay…. You don't have to get her." I pause, taking in a deep breath. "Yes, your question upset me."

Officer Johnson fades back into the corner, almost forgotten, as I stare into the eyes of Detective Donaldson. I search for any sign that she'd rather be somewhere else, but don't see it. Her attention seems completely focused on me. As if reading my thoughts, she leans forward in her seat, waiting for my next words.

"I guess we're close. He always says I'm special." My voice cracks on the last word. I hope I never have to use or hear that word again.

My stomach churns and my face burns in embarrassment.

The detective waits, staring directly at me. Finally she breaks her silence. "Can you tell me why he said that, Kat?"

The room starts to spin and Greg's words come rushing back. *Don't ever tell, Kitty Kat. They'll blame you. You're a bad girl, but I'll protect you. They'll never believe you. They'll call you a liar. They'll try to ruin our special relationship. You'll be sorry if you ever say a word.*

I flash back to the first time that I remember Greg calling me his special girl. He convinced me I was doing nothing wrong; just showing my love for him.

Mom and Dad were out somewhere with Jared. Greg was babysitting me and we were playing hide-and-go-seek. He wasn't dating Amy yet and Sarah wasn't born.

Greg said he had some fun new rules that we should try; that when he found me, I had to do something to show I loved him. And when I found him, he would do something to show he loved me. I thought it was a great idea because I loved Greg with all my heart.

The first time I found him, he gave me a kiss on the cheek. I did the same thing when he found me. The next time, the kiss on the cheek progressed to a kiss on the mouth. After that, Greg said that he wanted me to kiss him on the stomach. The next time, the kiss was lower.

That's when I became his special girl. "Kitty Kat, do you know how special you are?" he asked me that day. "You're my special girl now. We share a secret. This is a secret you can't tell anybody, not even Jared. If you ever tell, people will be very mad at you, and you won't be special anymore. If you tell, you'll be a very bad girl."

Tears rolled down my young, chubby cheeks at the thought of becoming a bad girl in Greg's eyes. He was the father figure that I always wished for.

Greg asked me if I understood, and I nodded my head so hard, I'm surprised I didn't kink my neck. Greg glowed with one of the special smiles he saved for me and told me that we should seal our secret together with another special kiss.

"Kat? Are you okay?" Detective Donaldson's voice snaps me back to the present. I stare at her absently, trying to clear my head of the memory. She hands me a tissue and leans back in her chair, as if she has all the time in the world.

When did I start crying? I dab at my eyes and blow my nose.

The detective folds my free hand into her warm one and squeezes. That single touch of encouragement and the moisture in her eyes is the final catalyst that bursts the dam inside me.

The words gush forth so quickly, I barely remember to stop at times to take a breath. What seems like an endless supply of tissues is handed to me, without my even realizing where it's coming from. I dab, blow my nose, and talk some more… dab, blow my nose, and talk some more.

Detective Donaldson holds my right hand the whole time. Occasionally, she asks a question for clarification, but she mainly sits there and listens.

I talk about everything from the time I became Greg's special girl, to him dating Amy and my jealousy, to them getting married, and Amy winning me over. I tell her of all the things Greg would say and do to me, and the things he insisted I do to him.

Finally I come to this past school year and all the turmoil I've been in with Jared leaving for school, fights with Steph, fights with Sarah, and worrying about Greg touching Sarah. I talk about my fading relationship with my parents, my confusion over Scott and my botched attempt at dealing with Greg.

At last, the room is silent. I lean back in my chair completely spent. My thoughts are empty. I don't remember a time without some horrible memory floating through my head, tormenting me. It's as if everything has been swept clean with the gush of words that poured out of me. The building could have been on fire and I think I would've still sat in this chair and continued with my story.

My head is lighter, my shoulders aren't slouched. The knot in my stomach is gone, as if a heavy burden has been lifted. I've gone through an exorcism and Greg has been purged from my system. *Is this what it's like to feel free?*

The detective's chair scrapes across the floor and she stands, bringing her finger to her lip while she thinks.

"We need to discuss a few things," Detective Donaldson says. "But first, I have to say to hell with standard protocol for a moment."

I'm engulfed in a warm hug before I have a chance to figure out what she means. Stunned, I'm not sure what to do, but then my arms wrap around her, seeking the comfort she's offering. I was right to trust her.

A sniffle from the corner of the room draws my attention

to Officer Jackson blowing his nose. I had forgotten he was even there.

Detective Donaldson releases me and sits down again.

"Now," she says rearranging the papers in front of her, "let's start by you calling me Mary. And Kat, I'm thrilled to meet such a brave survivor." She smiles at me. "I can't imagine the things you've gone through, or how you're feeling, but the abuse ends now, and we are here to help you."

I remain silent, eager to hear more. An inner glow starts to grow when I hear the word *survivor*. What a beautiful word. *I'm no longer a victim, I'm a survivor. I will fight this and I will survive.*

"Let's talk about help first, before we get back to the legal side of things. We have information here on arranging for counselling and they will also be able to recommend support groups if you feel that's something you want."

"I don't know…"

"Kat, don't decide right now. You probably feel like a ton of bricks has been lifted from you. Unfortunately, you aren't the first one to tell us a story like this. You've taken some major steps, but your healing will be a long process. You're going to need a lot of support over the next little while. This is going to be difficult, and once the shock of today fades, you may sometimes feel as if you have exchanged one burden for another."

I nod. "I'll think about it." I'd never really given a whole lot of thought to the fact that other survivors like me are out there. I always felt so lost and alone – so different and isolated from everyone else my age, except for Steph and Scott. I never thought about how I'd feel after talking to the police, either. Everything is suddenly very new.

"That's all I can ask, Kat. Now, let's talk about the legal side of this situation."

"Wh-What do you mean?" My heart stops. *Was Greg right? Am I in trouble now?*

Mary smiles and pats my hand. "Relax, Kat. You haven't done anything wrong. We will want to talk to your parents and ensure we have enough evidence for reasonable and probable grounds to make an arrest. With an arrest, we will be pressing criminal charges against Greg, meaning that unless Greg pleads guilty, this whole thing will go through the judicial system and possibly to trial. Cases like this sometimes get nasty with a lot of 'he said/she said.' Greg will be presumed innocent, until proven guilty. It will be your word against his."

Sweat beads form on my forehead. What will people say about me? How will my family and friends feel? The kids at school will look at me in the halls and they will know the disgusting things I did with Greg. Blood rushes to my head, pounding relentlessly, matching the beat of my heart.

"I…I don't think I can do that," I whisper.

"I know it sounds frightening, but just think about how far you've come. He should be punished for what he did to you. You'll spend a very long time recovering from this, Kat, and he doesn't deserve to walk around free. Consider the fact that he may have done this to others, and there could be more victims in the future unless he is stopped."

I've been concerned about Sarah and what might happen

to her. What if there were others? Do I have the power to stop him?

Maybe I'm not brave enough to be a survivor after all.

Chapter Twenty-Four

Mom's hold on my hand is like a death grip, but she remains quiet as we walk to the van, a few steps behind Dad.

When I came out of the room, Mom was pacing, obviously worried and agitated. Dad was sitting on a bench, scowling. Detective Donaldson spoke to them quietly, asking some additional questions. Since then, Dad hasn't said a word to either of us.

Mary gave me her card with her extension at the station, her cell phone number, and her e-mail address. She even wrote her personal e-mail address on the back in case I need to talk more, "off the record." She told me that he might not be a serial killer or a bank robber, but that Greg's a dangerous criminal all the same. She also told me that no decent person would ever blame me or look badly on me.

She gave me a lot to think about. Everything has happened so fast.

Mom hits the button on the key remote to unlock the van doors so Dad can get in. I stop her after Dad climbs into the side door of the van.

"Has he said anything at all?"

"Not really. You know how he is." She puts her hands to my cheeks. "Are you okay? I was so worried about you, and I'm so, so sorry about all this." I nod, but stare at the ground, disappointed that Dad didn't seem very concerned about me. I figured he'd at least ask Mom what happened when he was taken away and if I was okay, but he didn't.

Dad's head pokes around the van door. "Are you coming, or not?"

Sighing, I get into the van. Dad winces when he puts on his seat belt.

"Are you okay, Dad?"

"I'm fine. I forgot about that nasty right hook Greg has. Last time I felt that was in…"

Mom pulls out of the parking lot, the silence in the van thick and uncomfortable, until Dad finally clears his throat.

"What did you tell them, Kat?"

I take a moment to gather my thoughts before answering. Dad has a tendency to analyze and pick apart anything a person says, especially when the person is me.

"I told them the truth, Dad."

"I wish you had let me come in there with you. You need a lawyer present when you talk to the police. They can use anything you say against you."

"Mary was very nice, Dad. I don't think she'd do that. Besides, I haven't done anything wrong. They will use the things I said against Greg, not me."

"David, please," Mom tries to interrupt.

"Neither of you realize how things like this work." Dad waves away Mom's protests. "I'll call someone I know at the Crown Attorney's office and make sure this whole thing is handled properly."

Something inside me snaps. After everything I've been through, he's worried about a case. He can't stop being a lawyer for one moment to show me that he's my father first and foremost.

"No."

"Did you say no?" Dad's voice is filled with surprise.

"Yes. I don't want you to do that. I don't want you to be a lawyer. I want you to be my dad."

I stare out the front window, tears running down my cheeks. By now I should be like a dried up old prune with no more moisture to shed, but more tears fall.

"Katrine, I don't know how else to deal with this." I have to strain to hear Dad's words, not sure if I'm hearing correctly.

I turn in my seat to look at him. A tear slides down his cheek. I stare at it, mesmerized.

"It's the only way I know of to help you. Did Greg…did he…?" It's not hard to guess what Dad is trying to ask me.

"Greg did some awful things, Dad."

"Did he...Did he hurt you?"

How do you answer a question like that? He hurt me emotionally. Sometimes it would hurt physically as well. He would lie and threaten, and other times he'd be really nice and call me special and make me feel loved. He'd be the father figure I needed, and then he'd be the terrible, mean person I was afraid of. He'd understand me when I was feeling down, but then he'd take advantage and make me do things I didn't want to do.

Dad seems to accept my silence as affirmation. "He's my best friend. I trusted him with my family. I don't understand. I just can't believe it."

Immediately defensive, I shout out that I am *not* a liar, and if he doesn't believe me that he isn't much of a father.

Dad looks stunned. The van jerks sideways as Mom jumps, startled by the sudden rise of my voice. Tears are running down her cheeks, too.

"I didn't mean...that's not what I meant, Katrine." Dad looks into my eyes. "I know you're not lying. I know it in here." Dad pats his chest over his heart. "He just betrayed us all. I feel so stupid. He even had a wife, and they wanted children so badly. Amy...what about Amy? You say she's gone. Is that true?"

I nod, sad that Amy has left town and we may never see her again. "She found my journal. She said she had to leave – she needs time away. She doesn't know if she'll ever be back."

"I guess I can understand that. If I feel like a stupid fool, I can't imagine how she feels right now. I'm…I'm so sorry, Kat."

I nod, not knowing what to say. I don't think I have ever heard the word *sorry* come out of Dad's mouth before.

"I didn't know. I failed and didn't protect you. I can never make that up to you."

I reach back between the seats to hold Dad's hand. "You just did."

We sit in silence while Mom pulls the van onto our road. Darkness is starting to fall and the front windows of the houses we pass are lit up from inside.

Dad grunts as he shifts his weight, reminding me of the fight. "What's going to happen to you, Dad? Are you being charged for the fight?"

"Don't worry about me, Kat. I'll work it out." For once, I don't even care that he has avoided giving me a direct answer. I've never been as grateful for my family as I am now, and I never thought I'd see the day that Dad and would I connect like we just did.

Mom pulls into our driveway.

Dad and I step out of the van. "What about Sarah, Kat? Did he do this to her as well?"

"I don't think so. I've tried not to let him be alone with her."

Mom closes her door and locks the van, joining us on the driveway. "You know, even if he hasn't, he would probably have started. You stopped him, Kat."

Dad unlocks the front door of the house, and turns to

put his hand on my shoulder. "I hope you know that Mom and I will support you all the way. This isn't going to be easy."

Another floodgate opens inside me, and I start crying again. I never realized how badly I wanted to hear words like that from my father until he said them.

Dad folds me in his arms and gives me the kind of hug I've been longing for since I was a little girl. But I don't feel like a little girl now. I feel like a young woman who is loved and supported. I'm not angry with Dad for failing to protect me from Greg. Greg had us all fooled. He was a master manipulator and he betrayed the people who trusted him the most: me, Mom, Dad, and Amy.

Chapter Twenty-Five

Scott and Steph rush out to join us on the front porch, anxiety in their eyes.

"You're okay?" Scott asks, looking back and forth at me and Dad.

I smile at Scott. "I'm fine…." He steps toward me, then stops and glances at my father.

"Gads, Kat, we're glad you're back. We were so worried." Steph steps past Scott and embraces me in a huge hug. I pull away from the suddenness of her embrace, caught off guard and not sure how I feel toward her at the moment.

"Is Sarah okay?" my mom asks.

"We finally got her to sleep," Scott says. "She was so upset;

it took us a while to calm her down. She's pretty confused and angry."

"She's not the only one," I say. "Sarah idolized Greg. I'm sure she'll have lots to say to me tomorrow."

Dad puts his hand on my shoulder. "Your mom and I will talk to Sarah. This is not your fault, and we'll make sure she understands that."

I glance at Steph. She smiles, as if unsure of our friendship after I pulled away from her hug. Some aspects of our relationship have changed. We are two different people with different thoughts and directions in life. I know we're still friends, but it will never be the same. I can deal with this, though. I think we can learn to accept each other the way we are.

I reach out and Steph steps forward into my hug. "Thanks for being here," I whisper.

"I wouldn't be anywhere else," she whispers back.

"Do you...do you know everything?"

Steph's back tenses and I release her to look into her eyes. She seems embarrassed for a moment, but then she smiles slightly and nods. "Sarah was confused. She heard some things that were said and was asking me questions. I didn't know what she was talking about at first, so Scott distracted her."

Scott grimaces while Steph continues. "I kind of attacked Scott after Sarah fell asleep, demanding to know what was going on."

Scott glances over sheepishly. "I'm sorry. It wasn't my place to tell. I tried not to say much."

I step away from everyone and look out over the front

porch. *So this is the way it's going to be? Word will spread because somebody heard something and someone else is willing to fill in the details for them?*

Oh, no. What have I done? How can I look at people without wondering if they know what I let him do to me? All the kids at school, the teachers, Aunt Sheila…will they all know my secret?

Uncontrolled panic blurs my vision, causing me to sway. *I've lost control. The only thing I had control of for all those years was my secret. It was mine and nobody else's, and now it's gone. Oh no, oh no, no, no.*

"Kat? Kat, answer me."

Is that somebody calling my name?

"Katrine." Dad's firm voice breaks through the haze. Someone is gripping my arm. I glance down to see Dad's strong hand holding me steady. I'm still dizzy.

"Dad?"

"Oh, Honey. Are you okay?" Mom steps forward, brushing hair away from my face with her hand.

I collapse into her arms. "What have I done, Mom? I can't…I can't do this. I can't face everyone."

Dad leans close and whispers in my ear that everything will be okay. "We'll be here with you, every step of the way. If this goes to court, the judge will likely order your name to be withheld. He'll order a publication ban so that your name isn't known to the public."

Mom steps closer. "Kat, we love you. You aren't going to go through this alone."

"I just wanted it to stop. I've hurt both of you, and Amy

too. I just wanted it to stop, and now…" I glance at my father. "He wasn't always bad. I shouldn't have done this to him."

"No, Kat, he wasn't always bad." He looks away for a moment and sighs. "He wasn't always good, either. And I want you to remember something. You didn't do anything to him. He's the one who broke the law. He put himself in this situation."

Dad gives me a small smile and leans down to rest his forehead against mine. He stares into my eyes and I will myself to believe him.

Chapter Twenty-Six

Scott and I sit on the front steps, lost in our own thoughts. I'm so tired that I don't think I could stand if I wanted to.

It's hard to believe so much happened yesterday. Just like that, my life has changed. My secret doesn't belong to me anymore. It has taken on a life of its own and will change the lives of so many people. Nothing will ever be the same again. On the other hand, Greg won't be able to threaten me anymore. The abuse has stopped. That's definitely a change for the better.

Detective Donaldson is supposed to call today to let us know what happened with Greg after we left the station. She assured me that once he is charged, he won't be allowed anywhere near me or my family during this whole process. That's a huge relief.

"You okay?" Scott asks.

"Yeah. Just thinking…." I try to stifle a yawn, but it escapes.

"Didn't sleep much, huh?"

I shake my head.

"Look, Kat…I know you have a lot to deal with. I couldn't sleep last night, either. I'm…well, I'm sorry. I feel really awful. This would have never happened if I hadn't attacked Greg last night."

"I don't know, Scott. Maybe it wouldn't have happened last night, but it would have come out in the open soon. I wanted it to stop so bad, I was like a time bomb. Something would have triggered an explosion."

I watch some leaves swirl through the air as they fall from a nearby tree.

"Maybe I just needed a bit of a push," I whisper, watching a red leaf dance over the ground before finally coming to rest.

"That's probably not the help you needed."

I shrug indifferently. "It's done."

"Kat, I've been thinking about what you said before you went to the station. You said something about having power. Maybe that's why guys like him do what they do."

"I guess so," I mumble.

"Yet they don't realize how much power they give to the kids they hurt."

"What do you mean?"

"Well…they have the power as long as the kid keeps quiet. But really, it's the kid with the control. Once the kid tells the secret, it's the kid who controls both of their lives."

"I suppose. But I don't feel like I'm in control."

"You took control back by taking his away."

"Maybe. But dealing with people and court and everything…I'm so scared, Scott. I don't feel any control at all. I'm just so scared."

"I know. But I'll be with you through it all. I promise."

Scott's words are soothing and comforting and provide some courage. What would I do without him?

"Kat…I need to talk to you about something."

"What?"

"I've been kicking myself since that day in the clubhouse when you told me what happened to you. I've been selfish over the last few months."

I open my mouth to protest, but Scott holds up his hand.

"I wasn't a good friend to you," he continues. "I was worried about my own problems. That's why I want you to know I'm here for you now, no matter what."

"Well, it did kind of seem like you were avoiding me at times," I say.

"I was."

"Why?"

"Kat, what he did to you rips me apart. I've never felt as violent toward another human being as I do toward Greg. Images of it haunt me at night when I try to sleep. I want to help you, but don't know how. "

My heart pounds with dread and anticipation as I struggle to understand what Scott is trying to say.

"I want you to know that, no matter what you say next, this won't change: I will stand beside you and support you."

"Scott?"

"I…I need to explain why I was avoiding you."

I nod. "Okay."

"I have feelings for you, Kat. I have a hard time thinking of you as a friend. I lo—"

"Stop!" I hold my hand up like a stop sign. "I'm not ready to hear something like that, Scott. Too much has happened in such a short period of time."

Scott winces. "I'm sorry. I shouldn't have said—"

I cut him off again. "It's okay. I'm glad you explained it. I didn't understand what was going on. I really missed you." I smile at him. "You *were* there for me when I needed you, though. When I lost my journal, you were there. You were my rock. It was almost like you knew how much I needed you, so there you were."

Scott glances down at the step.

"I just need time to sort out all these new feelings. Too much is happening right now. If you had told me a week ago that my secret would be out, my dad and I would finally connect, the police would be filing charges against Greg, and I'd probably never see Amy again…well, I would have thought you were totally crazy."

Scott smiles.

"So much has changed. A week ago, I wasn't ready for all this. I wasn't ready until today. I'm glad you're here to help me face what tomorrow brings. I'm going to need you." My voice cracks a bit.

I rise up from my perch on the step and Scott follows. Standing on tiptoe, I kiss him on the cheek. Wondering what it would feel like to kiss somebody as sweet and nice as Scott instead of Greg, I close my eyes and move my lips over, toward his. The contact is brief but thrilling. Sweet feelings of peace and happiness fill me.

When I open my eyes, Scott is staring at me, a wondrous look on his face. I might not be ready yet, but our day will come, just like this day eventually did.

"Until our today," I whisper to Scott, then turn and walk through the front door, a survivor, ready to begin the next part of my journey.

Acknowledgments

This book would not have come about without the help of many people. I especially want to express my heartfelt gratitude to my family – Willy, Karlyssa, Shalyn, my parents, and Brandon. Without your love and support, I would not be where I am today.

Thanks to Kevin McColley who assisted me with the initial manuscript through a course at the Institute of Children's Literature, and to my Blue Crayons critique group.

Special thanks to Second Story Press for taking on a story of this nature and realizing the importance of helping those who have suffered sexual abuse. Thanks to my editor, Kathryn Cole, whose feedback and guidance was invaluable, and to

Carolyn Jackson, the Managing Editor, for her feedback and support.

Although this book is fiction, I've drawn on some of my personal experiences with mental and sexual abuse. If this book can help one person, perhaps it will give what happened to me some purpose.

About the Author

PAM FLUTTERT lives in New Hamburg, Ontario with her husband and two daughters. In addition to writing and drawing in her spare time, she works at the University of Waterloo. Pam spends as much time as possible with her family, two dogs, and two horses. *Until Today* is Pam's first book. Writing it proved to be a therapeutic experience for her, and she hopes for some of her readers as well.